Withering Rose

Praise for Gathering Frost, the first book in Once Upon A Curse!

"My favorite thing about this book is the action. Jade isn't a sleeping princess. She's the best fighter and so fierce in her "empty" state. I felt like this was an urban fantasy with all the steam of a romance."
- Jessie Potts, *USA Today 'Happy Ever After Blog'*

"Davis writes with confidence and poise, and the story's many twists and turns stave off predictability and allow readers to become immersed in a starkly magical world filled with last hopes."
- *Publisher's Weekly*

"Gathering Frost is just awesome in every way. Beautiful prose, lots of heart-wrenching emotion, action and romance, a great, unstoppable villain, and a smart, tough heroine who will fight for what she wants."
- *Geeks In High School*

"It's well thought out and it unbelievably magnificent. I seriously couldn't put it down. Wait I never actually put it down. I started and finished in one sitting because it's just that good. This one is a MUST READ."
- *Happy Tails and Tales*

Withering Rose

Once Upon A Curse Book Two

Kaitlyn Davis

All Works By Kaitlyn Davis

Once Upon A Curse
Gathering Frost
Withering Rose
Chasing Midnight

Midnight Fire
Ignite
Simmer
Blaze
Scorch

A Dance of Dragons
The Shadow Soul
The Spirit Heir
The Phoenix Born

A Dance of Dragons – The Novellas
The Golden Cage
The Silver Key
The Bronze Knight
The Iron Rider

To my family for their unconditional love,
my friends for their overwhelming support,
and my fans for their incredible enthusiasm.
Thank you from the bottom of my heart.

One

I'll never forget the exact moment I started to die.

The day the world fell apart.

The day my world fell apart.

The morning of the earthquake began as a morning like any other. The air was cool and crisp, blowing through the slightly ajar carriage window and stinging my nose. I sat beside my father, hands encased in delicate lace gloves and folded perfectly on my lap. The dainty gold crown marking my station was pinned neatly into my hair, nothing compared to the brilliant, jewel-adorned one atop my father's tanned brow. I sat with my ankles crossed, trying my best not to kick my feet, though they dangled a foot above the carriage floor. And my eyes were glued out the window, transfixed by the snow-capped mountains cutting through the horizon like a sharp blade.

The mountains of the beasts.

A place of legend and myth.

The night before, I had overheard my father's guards telling stories about the bear king and wolf queen who roamed those jagged peaks, rulers made of flesh and fur. They thought I had been sleeping, as a proper princess would have been. But though I was a princess, I loathed being proper.

"Omorose?" my father asked, pulling me from the view that was beginning to make my heart thud in my chest.

"Yes, Papa?" I murmured.

"I'm not used to such silence from you. Are you nervous?"

I bit my seven-year-old lip, trying to ignore the flurry of butterflies that suddenly zipped across my chest. Was I nervous? Yes. Would I admit it? No.

I shook my head demurely. "No, Papa."

"The prince will still be the same boy you met before."

I nodded, swallowing. The prince was Prince Asher. My friend. A boy I had met a handful of times. But now I would be meeting him in a new light—as my betrothed. The contract was signed. And even as a young girl, I knew the gravity of that decision.

Prince Asher, son of the Ice Queen, the woman without feeling, the woman whose magic was to steal the emotions of everyone around her, the woman who ruled a desolate, heartless kingdom. My mother's magic was beautiful, filled with light and life. The magic I would inherit was beautiful. But the magic Asher would inherit was cold and scary and unfeeling, and it made me shiver just thinking about being married to a man with such power. I remembered him in my thoughts as a kind, lonely boy, who liked to dream and play as much as I did. But would he always be like that?

"Omorose?" my father prodded, reading my heavy thoughts—far heavier than a girl's of my age should have been. But being royal left little room for a normal childhood.

"I just miss Mama and sissy," I mumbled, lips wobbling, not needing to use too much energy to convince him of the truth of my words.

"Your baby sister is still too young to travel, but you'll see them both soon."

He patted my hands gently, a loving, worried touch.

And then our world shattered.

The ground shook, and we toppled, flipping end over end as the carriage rolled from the dirt road, smashing against the ground. I screamed as my body floated in air for an instant before slamming against the hood of the carriage, which was somehow now the floor. My vision went black as my head hit the heavy, gilded wood.

Everything faded.

"Omorose," my father was pleading. "Omorose!"

His hands caressed my cheeks, a light kiss pressed against my temple, and then my eyes flickered open. The dull ache in my head grew as soon as the light hit my pupils, blinding me.

"Omorose," my father cried, clutching me to his chest.

I glanced over his shoulder, trying to understand what had happened. The snow-covered fields were a mess of dirt and ice, shaken apart by godly hands. The mountains in the distance were haloed in rings of flurries and dust. The carriage was by our side, broken into pieces. One of the guards was covered in blood, lying still against the ground. Two more were looking beyond me, behind me, with an expression quivering between awe and alarm.

"Pa..."

I trailed off as I spun, my father still holding me tight.

I gasped, unable to breathe as a fear I had never known washed over me.

Gone was the dirt road.

Gone was the snow-kissed field.

Gone was everything I had ever known.

A city in chaos rested a few feet away from my frozen body. I didn't know what anything was at the time, everything was foreign and loud and unfamiliar. The only thing I recognized were the sounds of human screams and the sight of human tears. But everything else—impossible. I know now that what I saw were cars and cell phones and office buildings. I know now that the clothing I was startled by were jeans and sweatshirts and down jackets. I know now that the sounds blaring in my ears were car alarms and fire trucks. But at the time, I was overcome by panic and confusion, overcome by the otherworldliness of it all.

And then the very thing I feared most in my life happened.

I felt a tingle in my heart.

A warm, powerful tingle.

And it moved across my chest, down my arms, over my stomach, around my legs, spreading heat and strength across my entire body.

"Papa!" I cried.

No.

I didn't want it.

Not yet.

He met my eyes and instantly he knew that the shriek in my voice wasn't because of the unknown scene before us. It was the panic of my inheritance coming all too soon.

Pain flashed over his umber eyes.

Pain and hurt and a longing I will never forget.

But before I could say anything, before I could apologize for taking any ounce of hope he had left, the trickling heat exploded in my chest as the magic washed over me.

My mother's magic.

And the fact that it was now becoming mine could only mean one thing.

She was dead.

I tried to cry, to scream, to do anything to express the despair breaking my tiny heart apart. But I was lost in the burn of the magic as it funneled into me from some invisible place, pushing and pulling against my body, burying itself deep inside.

I distantly remember hearing a low voice shout foreign words. Through eyes that felt not my own, I remember seeing two blurry figures in blue pointing weapons at us, yelling at the two royal guards behind us, forcing them to drop their swords. They ordered my father the king around in a way no one dared before, shouting, using hand gestures when he didn't understand. My father listened, standing when they told him to, holding my limp body in his arms, refusing to let go. He walked and walked and walked, holding me silently. He only said three words the entire time the foreign men led us deeper into their unknown world.

"Don't use it."

And I knew what he meant.

Don't use the magic. Don't show them what we are. But more than that. Something deeper. Something only the members of my family knew, a secret we held close to our hearts. Because that moment, still as death in my father's arms as my mother's magic raged through me, that was the exact moment I started to die.

I felt it as the torment of heat and strength and power finished devouring my seven-year-old body. The fire ebbed.

Delightful coolness sprung to my toes, covering my body in a blanket of much-needed ice as the magic settled into its new home. The last place the warmth lingered was down in the center of my chest.

One moment, I was a happy, healthy child.

And the next, I was slowly beginning my descent toward death.

Because my magic came with a price. A curse my family had kept secret for generations. We had the power to give nature life, but only at the cost of our own. And as the heat finally disappeared, I felt the bloom blossom in the very core of my soul, a rose just like my name—a ticking clock hidden behind a façade of beauty.

From that moment on, my life would become a countdown, and all I could do was wait and watch as the petals of time slowly started to fall.

Two

Ten years have passed since the day that changed everything. Ten years of pretending to be something I'm not. Meek. Powerless. Just like everyone else. I've grown so tired of pretending.

But as I walk through the concrete halls of the underground base, I keep my head down. I try to remain invisible. I hug my books close to my chest, keep my eyes on the floor, and try to be as small as I can be. As unnoticed as I can be. But there are always eyes that watch me nervously, tinged with a bright spark of accusation I've done nothing to deserve. In these halls, being born in the magic world is all it takes to be considered other, different, strange.

Ten years ago, on the day of the earthquake, my father and I and our two guards were thrown into a foreign world we've been unable to escape. Earth. A place with no magic. A place where magic is considered the most evil thing of all. At first, the people of this world weren't sure what to do with us. Our clothes placed us as otherworldly. We didn't speak their language. So they locked us away, giving us just enough food to get by, speaking to us each day as though we understood. Eventually, their language became more familiar to me than my own. And after a year in captivity in a broken city I could only see through the bars on our window, when my father could finally explain himself and offer a truce, they moved us here.

They call it the Midwest Command Center, a freedom fighter base where the people of Earth fight with all they can to rid this new world of magic, to make it more like the world they remember. My father became their biggest source of information about our old world and the magic that lived there. He gave them our secrets to keep me safe. He pretended to hate the magic of our world, he devoted himself to helping them fight it, all so they would never guess what I was. What I could do. And at first, I thought it was our salvation. They allowed us to live in a house together. I could see the sun each day, could feel the wind on my cheeks. I had more freedom than I'd ever had before, even in the old world. No maids. Only two guards. No responsibilities except to be a child.

And then it all changed.

Magic isn't docile. It doesn't do well waiting in the background.

Every day became more of an internal struggle to keep my power contained. Every breeze carried the scent of the flowers I could grow with the twitch of my finger. Every weed breaking through stone whispered to me to turn it into something beautiful. The sun on my cheeks was a warm reminder that its light was not the only thing that could give plants life. I could give life. I could make things grow.

The magic swelled, pressing painfully against my chest, my fingertips, my toes, aching to be released, aching to be used. The power was a foreign presence inside of me with its own needs and desires, its own demands. And every time I took a breath, the magic came alive, fighting against my futile efforts to keep it contained.

My father commanded me to keep it inside.

But I lost control.

One night while I slept, the magic seeped out against my will. It had become too big for my little body to contain any longer. And when I woke in the morning, gasping as I felt the first petal in my soul fall away, the first reminder that using my magic cost me some of my own life, I still couldn't help but smile as the view of flowers filled my vision. A hundred different kinds, a hundred different shades. My inheritance. My birthright. The one little piece of my mother I could hold on to, that no one could take away. I laughed as I danced in the meadow my bedroom had become. My magic was beautiful. And having been used, it was satiated and calm, no longer fighting against me. The magic and I were both at peace for the first time since coming to this foreign world.

Then my ears caught the distant drum of an alarm ringing ugly against my wondrous morning. The pound of feet tearing up the staircase yanked me from my reverie. My father ripped open the door.

"I didn't mean it, Papa," I whispered.

"We have to get rid of it," he said harshly. Not angry with me, I knew, but still, the words hurt. "They have machines, Omorose. Machines that track the magic, that know when and where it comes from. They sensed the surge of your magic overnight. They're on their way here right now."

Together we ripped the flowers off the walls, tugged the roots from the floor, and stuffed the broken petals in my closet. Tears started to fall. I didn't have the strength to wipe them away.

When the freedom fighters came, the room was clean. My father told them it was the beast from the mountains, the one whose magic these freedom fighters were constantly tracking. He said the beast had come to kidnap me in the night, that he knew we were from his world, and he wanted to kill us for fighting against him.

The general and his men believed my father. They trusted him.

It saved my life.

And it destroyed it.

That day, my father moved us from our house. He packed our belongings and brought me to the underground section of the Midwest Command Center, a place no sunlight and no life could touch. A concrete box hidden in the dark. And I've been here ever since. Hiding. Pretending.

I can't remember the last time I truly saw the sun.

But each day I learn more about my new universe. The scientists who work here called our world a parallel one to Earth, similar yet different. And they say that long before the earthquake, something happened to throw one of our worlds off course and send it crashing into the other. Ten years ago, our worlds merged, becoming a patchwork planet. I've seen the map at the center of the base, blinking lights outlining the land and sea, outlining a new world that was unnaturally created from two different ones. In some places, the difference is so stark—a mountain range that suddenly cuts off to flat plains, a gently curving beach that abruptly turns into a wide stretch of hilly lands. Old rivers have dried up. New ones have formed, cutting through towns that survived the earthquake only to be flooded and destroyed. The weather is still adjusting to the new world, unpredictable as the tides and winds change each year.

But there is one thing on the map that consumes everyone's attention, one feature that silently demands to be seen. Dozens of misty circles pulse haphazardly across the globe, obscuring the shorelines and the terrains, spots that are masked and void. It's the magic. Their machines work on electricity, and I've come to learn that magic and electricity were not made to mix. The electric currents cannot penetrate the magic, so all that is left in these areas is a hazy abyss signaling the unknown.

And that's why I must continue to hide, why I must be very careful about when and where I release my power. The magic cannot be contained forever. Once in a while, it demands to be let out, to be released. It is an animal caged inside of me, ripping me apart for freedom. Sometimes, fighting it is too hard. So I wait for ferocious storms, and when the lights in my room flicker, I know it's safe. In the dark of the night, I sneak to the surface where rain and wind whip around me, and I use it. When my magic forces the electricity in the base to shut off, silencing their blinking machines and winking out the lights, the people of Earth think it is no more than the storm. Those few moments are precious and short, not long enough for anyone to raise questions. And after the brief second where I no longer have to pretend, I sneak back down into my prison to continue the pretense.

So it's been for years.

And I can't see the end.

Which is why I walk now with my head down, clutching my books and ignoring the sideways stares that follow my every movement. I've traversed these gray, lifeless hallways more times than I care to count, and I don't need to watch where I'm going. My feet remember the path to my classroom, just as easily as my mind does. I don't stop until I reach the open door, pausing for a moment to scan for an empty seat before rushing to fill it. Only when I sit do I notice the vase of lilies on my teacher's desk.

I gasp.

Immediately, the magic surges, washing over me and demanding to be used.

I close my eyes, trying to steady my breathing.

Even from ten feet away, I sense every slowly decaying cell of those gorgeous flowers. Cut at the end, plucked from nature to sit in a glass container and look pretty for a few days, all the while slowly dying inside. I understand them. And the magic within me wants to fix them. All it would take is a single thought, one second of wishing it were so, and roots would sprout at the base of the stems, sinking to the floor, searching for dirt. I could give those lilies life.

I could.

But I can't. It would cost me too much.

After a few minutes of steady breathing, I'm able to pull my thoughts from controlling the magic. And a few more minutes later, I finally register my name being called.

"Omorose?"

Snickers.

Laughter.

The sound grates against my ears, and I open my eyes quickly, flicking my gaze around the room. The girls at the front bite their lips, looking back and forth between one another, giggling not so quietly.

I wish after so many years I could say I was used to it, that it didn't hurt.

But it stings. It always has.

"Yes?" I ask, voice quiet. In the old world, I was a princess, a ruler, a leader. Here, I'm a wallflower, always shrinking away. It's hard to make friends when I'm always pretending. It's hard to make friends when I know anyone in this room would kill me if they found out what I truly was.

"Have you heard anything we've been discussing or were you just asleep in your seat?" my teacher, Mrs. Nelson, asks.

I sink lower. "No," I murmur. "I didn't hear."

More teasing.

More laughter.

"We're discussing everyone's plans for after graduation," Mrs. Nelson urges, bringing her tone to a gentler place. "The year is half over, and this week's focus will be on compiling applications for jobs. The world needs more teachers, doctors, soldiers, engineers, and physicists, especially out here at the bases. But in some of the cities, there are different opportunities, like journalists, broadcasters, politicians."

I shake my head.

I've never thought of what I want to do after graduation. There is no after for me. I can't leave my father, not after everything we've been through. All I have are endless days of walking these halls until he is finally ready to leave, a day I fear will never come.

"Speak up," Mrs. Nelson commands.

"I, I don't know," I respond, feeling my cheeks heat as my peers continue to stare at me.

Mrs. Nelson holds my gaze a moment longer, waiting with a flicker of hope for me to be normal for once. After a moment, the flicker fades. Disappointment lines her irises, and she turns to the next student.

"Dean?"

He's the general's son. It's no surprise when he confidently says he wants to enlist and become a soldier in the war against the magic. I try to focus on his answer, to make myself present and pull myself away from my thoughts. But as I turn in my seat to watch him speak, a word filters into my ear.

"Freak."

A painful spike of heat shoots down my back.

I sit up straight. I don't turn around.

I know it's only worse when I give in.

"Freak." It comes again.

I can't help it. I snap, spinning to face Amanda and her cronies. She watches me with a sneer, curling her upper lip and daring me to respond.

So easy. It would be so easy.

I wouldn't even have to open my mouth. One thought and I could curl vines of ivy around her ankles, gripping her tight before throwing her across the room. I've imagined it a million times, daydreamed about the expression of shock on her face, the fear that would line her eyes, the knowledge that I was more powerful than she would ever be.

It takes all of my strength to curl my fingers into my palm, to hold the magic in and turn away.

"Ooh, I'm so afraid," she whispers again, voice triumphant. They all snicker at my expense, proud of themselves for besting me yet again.

I take a deep breath, swallowing the clog in my throat back down.

They're not worth it, I remind myself. Not worth the disappointment I would see in my father's eyes if I lost control. Not worth my life if the soldiers here discovered what I was. At least, that's what I repeat in the back of my mind for the rest of class, not paying attention at all to the lesson Mrs. Nelson planned, a lesson about a future I can never have.

And then we're dismissed at lunch. The next half of the day will be combat training, basic skills everyone our age is expected to know—everyone except me. I come from the magic world, and they don't trust me enough to train me. Oh, I'm allowed to go to school and learn from books. Literature, biology, history, all of that is fine. But they'll never willingly put a gun in my hand and teach me how to shoot. Little do they know I don't need one anyway.

"Hey!" A hand lands on my shoulder, stopping me. I turn, unable to keep my jaw from dropping as I look into Dean's bright blue eyes. "I'm sorry about before, with Amanda," he says, smiling at me encouragingly. "She can be a bit of a, well..."

He trails off.

But we both know what word was going to come next.

I shrug, trying to ignore the way my heart is pounding in my chest. Is it the brilliant color of his eyes? The fact that he's speaking to me? The fact that someone is being somewhat nice to me for the first time in years? I don't know, but warmth floods my cheeks, and I shake my head.

"Don't worry about it," I mumble. Internally, I curse. What happened to the girl I used to be? She was tough, wasn't she? She stood up for herself, didn't she? Is this who my father wanted me to become?

"Are you okay?" he asks, peering closer.

The urge to run takes over. In that instant, I realize I don't want his attention. I'm the girl I've become for a reason. I don't want the general's son learning my secrets, looking at me like I'm not invisible, gazing at me like a mystery to solve.

But before I can step away from his touch, another voice calls. "Omorose!"

My father.

Dean jerks his hand away.

I press my back against the wall.

Did we look like two teenagers in love?

Is that why my father's voice came out high-pitched with panic?

"I have to go," I whisper.

Dean looks at me for another moment. I don't want to like the interest in his eyes, yet part of me, deep down, does. "A few of us are going to the surface tonight if you want to come. Just to hang out, party a little, get away from the adults." He shrugs.

The surface.

I sigh, unable to stop the smile that spreads across my cheeks at the thought of going to the surface, of breathing in the fresh air, of shaking off the stale underground. The smile that also spreads a little bit at the idea of being included, at the idea that someone might miss me when I don't come.

Dean smiles too.

I grasp the moment tightly, locking it away in the corner of my mind.

And then I turn abruptly away without responding because I know I can't go with him, not ever. And I know it would only hurt me more to think for a second that I could. He's just like everyone else in this world. He wouldn't like me if he saw the real me. And I can play pretend with my life, but not with my heart.

I'm better off being alone.

"Omorose," my father says urgently when I reach him. "Follow me, something's happened. Something we can't discuss here."

Three

"What's happened, Papa?" I ask, ignoring his unspoken request for obedience.

He glares at me. "Not here."

"But—"

I stop speaking as alarms blare, drowning out the sound of my voice. My eyes go wide as I realize the panic in my father's voice wasn't from finding me with Dean. Something's happened. Something that must affect everyone on this base for the alarms to be sounding.

"Is it the beast?" I ask softly as we race down the halls in search of our underground apartment. That's our name for the mysterious king who resides in the mountains, the one whose magic the Midwest Command Center is responsible for tracking. He is at the center of the hazy circle closest to us on the map, the one we watch day and night for any changes. Some say his magic is to take different animal forms, wolf and bear and hawk. Some say he can hide in plain sight. Some say he rules an entire kingdom of shape shifters. And some say that we still don't know what his power truly is, because even with all of our technology, we've never been able to get close enough to find out.

In the old world, my people were afraid of those mountains and the beasts who watched over them. In the new world, I've found myself wondering which side of the fight I should really be on. After all, wouldn't these people label me a beast too?

My father strengthens his grip and pulls me ahead, not bothering to answer. I am still a princess and he is still a king, so I bite my lip and stay silent, finally adhering to his command. But if the alarm isn't about the beast, then what?

The ringing quiets down, and a static crinkle takes its place. Everyone who was moving stops. Trying to blend in, we stop as well, but I can feel my father's pulse thrumming with nervous impatience. And then the voice of the general takes over.

"I hope that got your attention," he says lightly. A deep chuckle reverberates through the speakers, and all around us people release the breaths they didn't realize they'd been holding. I scrunch my brows, glancing toward my father. The general sounds happy, elated. So why is my father so afraid?

"Today is a glorious day," the general continues, his smiling voice coming through loud and clear despite the crackling of the microphone. My father grips my fingers so tight his nail beds turn white. "Today, after a decade of fighting the magic that turned our world upside down, the people of Earth have finally been victorious."

Murmurs rise up around us, excited chatter.

The general pauses for effect, as though he can hear all the whispers spreading around the base, all the hopeful theories about what that victory might be.

I, on the other hand, can feel the color draining from my face. A knot has formed in the pit of my stomach, twisting tighter and tighter with each prolonged moment of anticipation.

"We've just received a report that the Northwest Command Center has taken down the queen they've been fighting for ten years. The magic vanished from our radars late last night, and it has been confirmed this afternoon that the queen is dead, and that with her death, the magic plaguing New York City has finally disappeared."

Cheers erupt from everywhere at once, drowning out whatever the general's next word might have been. Some people are crying, others are shouting, more are hugging and laughing and beaming with joy.

I meet my father's eyes.

New York City.

New York City.

Why does it sound familiar? Why have I heard it before?

The knot coils tighter.

My mind races.

I'm missing something. I know I am.

But I can't think straight. All I hear over and over again is, the queen is dead. The queen is dead. They killed her. And everyone is cheering for the sheer joy of that fact.

I clench my fists as the magic stirs deep inside of me.

I know in that moment that they would kill me without hesitating. I've thought it before. I've told myself that a hundred times, to keep my heart guarded, to keep my magic in control. But I never believed it until now. Freak. That's what Amanda and her friends have been calling me under their breath for years. Freak. That's what everyone who watches my father and me out of the corner of their eyes believes. I am a freak to them. An outsider. Someone who doesn't belong and never will.

The queen is dead.

But all I hear in my head is Omorose is dead. I am dead. My magic and my legacy are dead. All I hear in my head is their uproarious applause.

"Quiet down, quiet down," the general says between laughs. He's partaking in the merriment. And why wouldn't he? He's devoted his life to fighting magic, to fighting me.

No one is quieting down. In fact, they just get louder.

Someone next to us grabs my father, pulling him in for a hug. My father instantly turns off the panic in his face, flipping his expression to a jubilant smile, hugging the man and joining in with the cheers. He glances at me, expression pleading.

Blend in, his eyes are saying.

Pretend. Join in the revelry. Don't let them notice you are different.

"Quiet down!" the general repeats, still laughing.

Suddenly, his words sound like they are meant only for me. Quiet down. I've spent my entire life being quiet, looking down, bowing my head to keep everyone from noticing me. I can't do it anymore.

My father reaches for me, but I step back. I shake my head. I can't meet his eyes, can't stand to see his false happiness for another moment.

Instead, I flee.

Everyone is so consumed by their joy, they hardly notice me as I swerve my way between them, walking quickly but not running. The general keeps talking, but I'm not listening anymore. Blood pounds in my ears, and it drowns out everything else. Magic thrums through my veins.

When I finally reach my bedroom, I do the only thing I can think of doing to release my anger, my hurt, my frustration. I scream until I collapse on the floor. Then I scream again. And when my throat is too raw to scream anymore, I finally notice the salty tears dripping down my cheeks.

I crawl across my carpet and reach beneath my bed, using my shaking fingers to pull out the box I've hidden there—the box I haven't opened in five years. My heart skips a beat, and everything in the world turns peacefully quiet. As my breath becomes uneven, my throat clogs, growing tight.

I open the lid and pull out the torn, stuffed bear I hid inside.

Mr. Winky.

A gift from my sister.

It's the only thing I still have from my old world, my old life. The crown I was wearing on the day of the earthquake was confiscated, as were my family ring and the necklace my mother had given me—all jewels that could be sold for profit. My dress was thrown out when I grew too big. The trunks my father and I had packed for our journey had either vanished during the earthquake or were stolen from us. This little bear with a missing eye and patches on its seams was the only thing deemed not worthy enough to take, a toy no one had the heart to steal from a frightened child. And I'll be forever grateful for that fact.

I hug the soft fabric to my chest, letting Mr. Winky take my tears and my fears as my mind opens up to a memory I haven't allowed myself to think of in years. But no matter how much time passes, I will never forget the day my sister gave this to me.

It was the last day I saw my mother and her alive.

It was the last time I ever felt truly at peace.

The last time I ever felt that I belonged.

It was one week before the earthquake. I was standing in the courtyard outside our home, a grand castle at the very center of our kingdom. The carriage door was open behind me, and my father had already climbed inside, settling himself in for the start of our journey. But I was afraid. I was crying because I didn't want to go. I didn't want to have a fiancé, I didn't want to leave my mother and my sister for so long, I didn't want to grow up.

"Hush, darling," my mother whispered, kneeling down to my eye level as she wiped the tears from my cheeks. "You'll be a queen someday, just like me. You'll have magic, just like me. And Prince Asher will be your king, just as your father is to me. You will grow to love each other. And trust me, at this moment, I would bet he is just as afraid as you are."

I sniffled, lifting my chin to meet her gaze. "Do you really think so?"

She smiled lovingly. "I know so."

"How?" I whined.

"Because once I was just like you, a little girl afraid of what the future held for me. And then, just like you will, I learned how to be brave, how to swallow my fears and see each challenge as an opportunity for growth, as an opportunity to be a leader for my people."

I shook my head. "I'm not brave."

She cupped my cheek in her warm palm, rubbing the last tear away. Then she leaned forward and kissed my brow.

"My darling Omorose, you'll learn to be brave. And this journey with your father is the first step."

"Ro Ro," a little squeaking voice said from behind my mother.

I smiled at my little sister. She was barely two and still wobbly on her feet as she walked closer to me.

"Ro Ro brave," she said confidently.

I laughed. "Thanks, sissy."

But she shook her head as though she could sense the defeat in my tone. "Ro Ro brave!" she repeated adamantly, and then she held out her stuffed bear, an offering to me. It was the same bear I grew up playing with, the one I doubted she remembered that I had given to her on the day she was born.

"You keep Mr. Winky until I get back," I murmured, peeking at my mother to see her eyes shining proudly at both of us. I was trying to be brave, to be an example for my little sister just like Mother had told me to be. But my sister just shook her head and stomped her foot, even more stubborn than me, and held out Mr. Winky again.

"Take him with you, darling," Mother told me gently.

I grabbed the little brown bear, clutching him to my chest the way I used to when he was my toy. The soft touch of his fur was comforting, and he smelled like home. Then I hugged them both goodbye and climbed into the carriage next to my father. He wrapped an arm around me, pulling me to his side, offering the silent strength he knew I needed.

I tried to be brave as the carriage rolled away.

I didn't once look over my shoulder for one last peek of my mother, my sister, and my home.

But I wish I had.

As I hug Mr. Winky to my chest now, he still smells like the fresh garden scent of home. A place I will never see again. A place I hardly remember. But I breathe in the essence of the people I love, trying to form their images in my mind. My mother's wild auburn hair is easy to remember because I see it in the mirror every day. Her rosy skin, always a hint away from a blush, was the same as my own. But her face is harder to see. I remember her eyes, their mix of gold and green that reminded me of a sunny spring day. The rest is blurred. Did she have my nose? My chin? And what about my sister? What would she look like now? She was so little when we left. Her chestnut hair had barely started growing. Her eyes were green too, I think. Her skin was darker, like my father's. But what I remember most is the sound of her laugh, so intoxicating that whenever I heard it, I would laugh too, and together we would fall into a fit of giggles for no reason at all.

Be brave.

Those were their parting words to me.

And how have I honored that request? By hiding, by pretending my life away, by cowering in the corner. Even now, I'm locked away in my room, running from my fears instead of facing them.

No more.

I can't do it anymore.

It's time to be brave.

I'm not sure how long I sit alone in my room, hugging that old bear to my chest. But when the doorknob turns and my father's head pokes through, I finally have the courage to say the words I've wanted to say for so long.

"Papa, I'm leaving." A weight lifts from my chest as soon as they are spoken. And before my doubts can take over, I push through the fear and continue. "I want more than a life of hiding. I want more than a life of fear. I can't stay here anymore. I yearn for freedom, for adventure. I yearn to be myself, to find a place where I belong. So I'm leaving. With or without you, I'm leaving, and you can't stop me."

Four

He doesn't say anything. Instead, my father steps fully into the room and shuts the door behind him, watching me quietly. He traverses the small space quickly, sitting across from me on my reading chair, clasping his hands together on his lap.

He looks older than I've ever seen him. The wrinkles across his brow suddenly seem deeper. His hair suddenly seems grayer. And something in his expression is so unbearably forlorn that I need to look at the ground.

"I forbid it," he says with the deep voice of the king I remember.

My heart drops. But I lick my lips and find the strength to look up and meet his gaze. "What's keeping you here, Papa? What's keeping us here?" A brief glimmer of light passes over his eyes, and I recognize it. Hope. The heavy pressure in my chest grows. "They're gone, Papa. They're dead."

The light in his eyes fades.

His frown deepens.

A familiar despair gnaws at my thoughts, but I push it away. We've never spoken of this, but it's always been there. And it's time.

"Mother and sissy are gone," I whisper. My throat is still raw from my earlier screaming, so the words come out scratchy and broken. "Our kingdom is gone. How many times do we need to search the maps before you will believe it? Our castle, our city, our lands, they disappeared in the earthquake, and there is no way to retrieve them. You are king of a lost kingdom, and I'm the princess of a people who are never coming back. I can't live in the past any longer."

"We don't know," he whispers, strength gone.

I cringe. "We do, Papa. We've known for a while. How many more times will you use their machines to search in vain for our kingdom? How many more times will you try to find a home that isn't there? Mother died ten years ago, you and I both know that is a fact. I could never have the magic otherwise. And there's another fact we both know. Sissy was barely two, and Mother never let her out of her sight. They are gone, Papa. We must accept it. We must move on and figure out how to live in this new world we've been thrown into."

He looks to the floor, dropping his forehead into his hands, running his fingers through his ebony hair. For the first time in a long time, I realize I'm not the only one hiding, not the only one running. "You are all I have left, Omorose."

"I know, Papa," I murmur gently. "We're all each other has. And if you love me, you must realize it is killing me to be here. You must—"

"Being here is the only thing keeping you alive," he interrupts, snapping his head up to find my eyes.

My own go wide and I flinch as though struck.

There is a confession in those words, one I've never understood until now.

"You," I gasp, then swallow, trying to bite back the hurt. I shake my head as the realization fully hits. "Staying here was never about Mother or sissy or our people. Staying here, you knew what it was doing to me. You knew how hard it was for me. But you didn't care. As long as I couldn't use my magic, you didn't care."

"Your magic will kill you," he says, not denying anything. "I watched it kill your mother. Day by day a little bit of her life seeped away, a little bit of her soul, her happiness, her beautiful essence that I loved so dearly. You were too young to understand, but it's not only time the magic takes away. It strips away pieces of you, slowly enough that you won't even realize they're gone until it is too late."

"Papa," I whisper.

I know all of this. I've felt it.

"Twenty-five years." He sighs deeply. "Twenty-five years is the longest amount of time any woman in your lineage has lasted after inheriting the magic. Twenty-five years is not enough, Omorose. I've outlived one wife and one daughter, and I cannot do it again."

I deflate. My shoulders hunch, and the bear I had still been clutching to my chest falls away as my arms go limp.

Twenty-five years?

And I've spent ten of them in hiding.

I shake my head and take a deep breath. "This changes nothing," I answer softly. "If anything, it makes my conviction even stronger. I have to go, Papa. If I only have fifteen years left, I want them to be spent living. And what I do here? It's not living, Papa. I'm barely getting by, barely surviving. Don't you want more for me than that?"

The corners of his eyes glisten. But his jaw is hard-set and stubborn.

I continue before he can say anything. "Don't you want me to be happy?"

My voice falls away. The words hang between us, filling the small space of my room with a charged silence. I refuse to say anything until I have his answer. He refuses to answer me. Instead, we stare at one another, two sets of stubborn umber eyes, the only features I inherited from him.

"Where would you go?" he asks somberly. "Did you really think I haven't thought all of the options through?

There is nowhere in the world you could go where they wouldn't find you. Always their machines are pulsing, tracking every movement the magic makes around the world. Always they are watching for it. It is safer to be here under their noses than out there on the run with no food, no warmth, no protection. You are still a child, my darling Omorose, just a child. You don't understand what you are asking for."

My heart warms when I hear the endearment from his lips, the same one my mother used to use. My darling Omorose. Their darling. And I love his love for me, his concern for me. But I'm not a child, and I haven't been one in a very long time.

I've spent so long dreaming of escaping this place that an answer rolls smoothly off my tongue, one I've practiced a million times in my thoughts. "I'm going to find Queen Deirdre and Prince Asher. He's still my fiancé. He'll keep me safe. And no one will be able to tell I'm there. On their machines, the magic all looks the same. Once I'm in Queen Deirdre's realm, they won't be able to tell my magic from hers. They'll think it's the same. I have thought this through, Papa."

His brows furrow tightly and then lift as an almost apologetic expression passes over his face. He stands, crossing the small room quickly. The mattress dips below his weight as he hugs me to his side, sighing deeply.

"What?" I ask softly.

He kisses my temple. I look up at him, confused.

"Did you hear the announcement?" he finally says, voice so gentle I hardly recognize it.

"Yes," I say, breathing the word more than saying it as the wheels in my head start to spin. New York City. New York City. The name turns over as I shuffle through my thoughts, trying to place it.

"Kardenia," I whisper. "New York City is Kardenia."

My father nods.

Suddenly everything becomes clear.

"Queen Deirdre is the magic user they killed?"

My father nods again.

"And the magic is gone?"

"Yes," he confirms, gauging my reaction.

But I'm numb. For so many years, I'd been practicing my speech. My plan had been foolproof. How could my father deny me the right to find my fiancé? How could he refuse to let me go to a city where he knew I'd be safe? How could he prevent me from fulfilling a contract he himself signed a decade before?

"Asher is dead," I murmur.

And all my plans have died with him.

"I'm sorry, Omorose." My father hugs me tighter, but I can't feel it. My limbs have grown cold. "If the magic is truly gone, then we both know what must have happened. The last heir has to die for the magic to be released back into the world. Queen Deirdre was killed, her magic passed to her only heir, her son, and then he was killed as well. There is no other way to get rid of the magic, or your mother would have told me long ago. She would have done it to save you from her fate."

I can't think about my mother. It's too hard.

So I think about a different queen. "But Deirdre was undefeatable," I protest, shaking my head and pushing my father away. Adrenaline pumps through my veins. "Her magic was so strong. She could steal people's emotions. She could control their thoughts and their movements, could put suggestions in their mind. Loyalty was her power. How could anyone defeat that?"

"I don't know," my father says, shaking his head. There is still a hint of pity in his eyes, but mostly there is love. "The general said there will be more information coming in over the next few days. Some of the survivors are going to share their stories and reveal what they know about defeating the magic."

I pace across my flowery carpet, grasping in vain for another option, another plan, another chance at freedom. But my father is right—where could I go where they wouldn't find me?

And then I stop as though struck.

My feet are rooted to the ground.

My head turns toward the gray concrete wall of my room, but my eyes see beyond it. My gaze cuts through the underground, through the dirt and the iron and the rock, and remembers a view I haven't seen in years—the sweeping veranda my old room on the surface used to look upon.

The mountains.

Snow-capped peaks far off in the distance.

The sanctuary that has always been waiting within reach but I never considered until now.

"I can go to the beast," I mutter, speaking to myself.

But my father hears. "Absolutely not."

He stands, grabbing my arm, turning me away from the wall as though he too can see the vision filling my sight. But I spin in his hold, eyes wide with possibility.

"It's perfect, don't you see, Papa? We can tell them he kidnapped me. It worked years ago when I lost control, they believed when you said he wanted to take me for revenge. They never doubted you." My words are flowing at a mile a minute as the excitement mounts. My pulse races as the puzzle pieces begin to fall into place. The more I speak, the clearer everything becomes. "I'll run away. I won't use any of my magic until I reach the border where the beast's magic begins to affect the machines. They'll think it was him."

"Omorose," my father tries to interrupt.

But I can't stop.

I won't.

"There's a bunch of kids going to the surface for a party tonight. I'll go with them. I'll get separated from the group. Tomorrow morning, you tell them I never came home. I can leave some clues behind me, shred up some of my clothes. I can even cut myself if I need to. I can—"

"Omorose!" he shouts.

I only stop because I notice a tear falling slowly down his cheek.

"Omorose," he repeats, voice breaking. I can see the fear written across his face. Fear for me.

"He has magic, too, Papa. He won't hurt me," I say.

"You don't know that. You can't. The stories—"

"Are just stories," I finish for him. Then I reach up and wipe the drop from his deeply tan skin, meeting his watery gaze. "Those stories are from a different time, Papa. The world has changed. People with magic can't afford to be each other's enemies, not anymore. He'll help me, I know he will."

"Help you what?" he asks, tone full of the same dread that's written across his face.

I know what answer he wants to hear. It's the only answer that might make him agree to this plan. The only answer he'll accept. But it's also a lie. And it rolls smooth as butter through my lips. "Help me get rid of it."

Relief flickers in his cocoa irises.

I fight the guilt coiling in my gut. "If this is what magic has become, my death trap, my personal prison, I don't want it anymore. It will kill me slowly if I use it. My death will just be quicker if it's discovered. The only freedom I see for myself is the freedom I could have if the magic were gone. And the beast might know something. His magic might be able to help. I have to try. I have to do something."

The words are more heartfelt than I thought they'd be.

I'm no longer sure who I'm lying to.

My father.

Or myself.

"Okay," he whispers.

For a moment, I think I've imagined it.

But then he sighs, and his shoulders fall as though a weight he has been carrying around his entire life has been lifted. And maybe it has.

"Okay," he says louder, with more authority.

I jump into his open arms, and he catches me, just the way he used to when I was a little girl. Laughter rolls up my throat from a place I thought had died with the earthquake. I feel light, bubbly, like a child again. More than anything, I feel brave.

"Thank you, Papa," I whisper into his chest.

His grip tightens.

"I'll come back as soon as I can," I promise. "And then we'll both be free to find a new home together. A place where we don't have to pretend. A place where we don't have to live in fear any longer."

Five

It's after midnight by the time I've found enough nerve to leave my room and make my way to the surface. There's a quiver of excitement beneath the anxiety, a little part of me that is thrilled to finally go on an adventure. But the bigger part of me is shaking at the thought of leaving everything behind, of seeking out a man so terrifying we call him the beast. And there's another little piece of me, the wallflower piece I can't quite shake, who is just scared of the simple fact that I'm going to my first real party. And that when I'm there, I need to create a scene so embarrassing that no one will blink twice when I run away. But before any of that can happen, I need to make it to the surface, and I need to control my magic.

The last time I breathed in fresh air was five months and seventeen days ago. I always keep count. I always try to see how long I can push it before needing to use the magic just a little bit. The more I can keep it inside, the better off I am, because I never really know when a storm is going to pass through that is ferocious enough to affect the electricity, covering my tracks. But the older I've grown, the worse my control has become. Each time I use the magic, my addiction to it strengthens. Right after the earthquake, I was able to repress it for three years before that night in my sleep when it leaked out. And then three years turned to two, which turned to one. The last time I went to the surface, I had been holding the magic in for eight long months, and I was desperate for release. I was barely able to contain the power beneath my skin. Each breath was a struggle for those last few days. We'd been in the middle of a drought, and I was terrified a storm would never come.

My fingers still twitch at the memory. And as I turn down another long hallway, they keep shaking, more and more with each step I take toward the exit.

The only thing I'm thankful for right now is that there is no need to worry about getting caught sneaking outside. I've heard of some freedom fighter bases where everyone lives underground, where the magic they are fighting is so dangerous that they need to implement very strict rules just to ensure everyone's safety. But here, there is no need. Though we call him the beast, the most frightening thing about him is that we really don't know what his magic does. We live very close to the edge of where his magic stretches, but he's never tried to use it against us, not unless we go on the offensive first. So we live a relatively safe life. Safe enough that many of the people who live here still choose to live above ground. And tonight, everyone is celebrating. Some are drunk on preciously saved alcohol. Some are just drunk on joy. Everyone is wandering the halls, going up into the night and coming back down to the underground base. Disguised by so much activity, I don't look the least bit suspicious as I make my way slowly across the base.

Not yet, anyway.

But I will.

Which is why I wait until the ramp to the surface is empty before slowly making my way up the steep incline. The fluorescent lights buzz overhead, flickering unnaturally. The concrete walls press in against me. My boots thud against the thick floor.

I hate it down here.

So I keep my eyes glued to the solid metal door at the end of the tunnel, watching it grow bigger with each step as I try to ready myself for the onslaught. Breathe in. Breathe out. Step one foot. Step the other. I bring my body into a rhythm, clearing my mind, doing whatever I can to prepare.

Then, gently, I reach out and input the eight-digit code we are all forced to memorize at the start of each year. When the light turns green, I twist the silvery latch in the middle of the door, listening as the bolts slide free. I open it.

The smell of wet grass hits my nose.

I double over as my magic surges to life. A cry leaks out as my heart explodes, scorched by the magic as it forces its way out of the tiny hole I'd pushed it into. Heat courses painfully through my body, stinging and tingling, as though every part of me was numb and is suddenly being prodded painfully back to life. I shiver and twist. Every muscle clenches tight as I struggle for control, but I know I can't let it out. Not yet.

My senses expand as the magic begins to take over. I'm aware of each blade of trodden grass, every flower struggling in the early winter frost, all of the dead leaves scattered across the ground. I feel every stem stretching into the sky and every root seeping into the dirt. Nature overwhelms me with its glory.

I continue breathing slowly, focusing my thoughts on counting out each inhale and each exhale. Every time I come to the surface it is the same, and after so long, I've mastered the painful and unnatural process of keeping my magic inside. After a few minutes, I can finally stand.

I take a hesitant step, forcing my feet fully through the door as I close it behind me. The tunnel exits into an old abandoned cottage with shattered windows, which is why that grassy breeze slipped in so easily. The high-security door I just exited looks like no more than rotting wood on this side, an old closet door with its paint chipping off and rusted hinges. Even the keypad is disguised, hidden behind a crooked picture frame. No one would ever take notice of this old broken-down home, so it conceals the entrance to our base quite effectively.

Magic simmers beneath my skin as I make my way fully outside. I can't allow myself to get distracted for even a moment. Half of my attention must remain on controlling it. Sometimes, the magic is my friend. Sometimes it does what I want when I want it to. But at times like this, it feels foreign with a mind of its own, like another soul living inside of me, with a will and wants different from my own. Right now, it yearns more than anything to be released back into the world where it belongs.

I force a smile to my lips as I pass by people still celebrating on the streets. Some sit on their porches, talking loudly, strumming guitars. Others are quieter in their revelry, looking up at the stars and the moon, lost in their own thoughts. I try not to disturb them as I wander through, searching for my peers.

Though I've never been to one of these parties, I've overheard enough conversations to know where all the kids my age go to get away from adult supervision for a little while. I wasn't sure if they'd go there tonight or if they'd stay closer to the base where everyone was celebrating, but as I walk through our small aboveground town, I don't see a single teenager hanging around. So I wander past the last row of houses and follow the dirt path leading to our solar energy field.

Totally off limits, of course.

But that's what makes it fun, right?

I walk for a mile or so with only the moon to guide me before I finally see soft lights in the distance—rechargeable flashlights. We all have them stored in our rooms in case of emergency, not that this would exactly qualify. And then I notice the glinting ebony surfaces of the solar panels resting in parallel lines across the massive field, the most reliable source of energy for our base. I'm told in old Earth, people didn't have to worry about electricity too much. If you paid for it, it was there. But the earthquake messed with their power lines and grids, especially out here so far from major cities. Sometimes the adults talk about the old days when things like cell phones and televisions were considered necessities, not luxuries.

By the time I reach the fence, I can tell the party is in full swing. Someone must have hijacked access to an outlet because music mixes with laughter and muddled conversation, probably one of the old CD players we keep in the classroom. There's a lock on the gate, so I'm guessing Dean stole the codes from his father to sneak inside and get access to the grid. But everyone else is outside the fence on the far side of the field. I make my way over, trying to build my courage with each step.

I'm a princess. I have magic.

I'm about to run away into the realm of a beast.

And I'm afraid of a few mean girls.

I sigh and shake my head, trying to stop the butterflies soaring around my stomach at breakneck speed.

It's stupid, I know. But I've spent almost a decade pretending to be meek and afraid. I'm not sure I really know how to be anything else—not yet.

I've barely reached the edge of the party when a voice interrupts my internal pep talk.

"You came!"

I spin with my heart in my throat but relax as soon as I meet Dean's excited blue eyes. He found me quickly, so quickly it sort of feels like he might have been waiting for me. I try not to let that thought linger for too long. But it's nice to feel wanted, even if I know his want is really aimed toward a girl I'm only pretending to be.

"I came," I say softly, more like a sigh.

But he doesn't notice. He gestures to me to join the party, and when I walk too slowly, he meets me half way, falling in with my steps. "I'll admit, I never thought I'd see the day when Omorose Bouchene would come to a party."

"Me neither," I murmur, deciding on honesty as the best path.

"I'm glad you did." He smiles, and I can sense his eyes watching me, but I keep my gaze on the ground. It's better that way. "You want something to drink? We managed to sneak a bottle of rum and some orange juice out of the supply room."

I shake my head. But he's not discouraged at all by my silence.

"So why did you come?" he asks, tone curious.

"Because," I say, glancing up at him. "Someone finally invited me." An expression passes over his face that looks suspiciously like guilt. But that wasn't what I wanted. So before I realize what I'm doing, I reach up and place my hand on his arm, stopping us both. "I meant that as a thank you," I say quickly, unsure where the sudden burst of confidence is coming from. "Not so you'd feel sorry for me or anything. I'm not really used to people including me. It's a nice change of pace."

He grins.

I look back at the ground and let go of him.

"Is there any water?" I ask. My throat is dry.

"Oh yeah, sure, I'll be right back."

When he's gone, I realize that Dean wasn't the only one to notice my arrival. And without him close by, everyone finally has the nerve to gawk the way they wanted to before. There are about forty other teenagers at the base, and I think thirty-nine of them are watching me right now.

Heat floods my cheeks. I can't stop it. I've never been able to. And then almost against my will, my hands start wringing together, and I shift nervously from foot to foot.

Where'd Dean go?

And more importantly, where is—

"Omorose," an overly sweet voice calls. Amanda.

I stand my ground.

After all, this is the exact reason I came here. To give them all a show. To cause a scene. But it was a little easier when it was all in my head, and I can't find my voice quick enough to respond.

"What are you doing here, freak?" she mutters when she gets close enough that no one else will hear.

I know that all I need to do is fight back a little bit, just enough to make her feel for a moment like I'm a threat. And after that, she'll do the rest. But I still can't speak. I'm paralyzed.

"I..."

"You what?" she taunts. "Thought maybe someone here actually wanted to spend time with you? As if a few hours in class isn't enough to make us all want to barf."

Be brave, I tell myself.

Just for a moment. Just this once.

"Someone here does want to spend time with me," I whisper. Each word that passes through my lips gives me more strength, more fight. My voice grows louder. "Dean invited me. In fact, right before he went to go get me a drink, he told me how happy he was that I came."

For a moment, I really think her eyes are on fire they are so filled with rage. And instantly, I know that one sentence was enough, one brief moment of bravery was enough. Amanda's been selfish and territorial for as long as I've known her. Nothing would make her more furious than the idea that someone as weak as me would dare take something that belongs to her.

"You'd like to think that, wouldn't you, freak?" she spits. But before she can say anything else, Dean's voice halts her.

"Amanda," he calls. And he doesn't know it, but the little bit of warning in his tone seals my fate.

"Dean!" She turns, plastering a smile across her lips, gaining a flirty expression.

The party has gone silent. No whispers. No laughing voices. Nothing but the light music drifting through the forest.

We have an audience.

"What were you guys talking about?" he asks innocently, handing me a cup of water. I can't help but notice Amanda's gaze fasten on the spot where his fingers graze against mine.

"Oh, just girl stuff," she responds lightly, mysteriously enough that he'll ask a follow-up.

"Oh, yeah? Like what?" He's predictably intrigued. But also wary, I'm happy to note.

She giggles. "I can't tell you." Then she looks at me pointedly. "They're not my secrets to spill."

"What secrets?" he asks, turning to me with a slightly confused expression.

I take a sip of water and mumble, "I don't know what she's talking about."

But a trickle of fear seeps down my spine. What does Amanda know? Could she have possibly found out what I truly am? How could she have uncovered any of my secrets? What is she talking about? What's her plan?

"You don't have to be shy," she says encouragingly, as though we're suddenly best friends.

I watch her, wide-eyed and unsure.

She nudges me with her shoulder, as though prodding me to confess.

My throat is clogged up. I shake my head.

She rolls her eyes. "It's not a big deal, really. She was just telling me how excited she was that you invited her out here, sort of like a date almost. She was hoping you might give her, well, her first kiss. I mean, Dean, you must know she's been in love with you for years."

Dean glances at me and then quickly looks away.

But it takes a moment for the full force of Amanda's words to reach my ears because I'm so relieved that the word *magic* hasn't rolled off her tongue. She doesn't know my secrets. She doesn't really know how to destroy me.

But then someone snorts under his breath.

I hear the hum of swiftly spoken whispers.

The light chime of laughter.

Victory shines brightly in Amanda's eyes right before she contorts her face into a convincingly shocked expression. "Oh god, don't tell me you didn't know, Dean." She glances my way. "I'm so sorry. I didn't mean." And then she looks back at him. "I really am sorry. I didn't think it was a secret, not really."

I look at Dean, knowing my cheeks are on fire, and there's nothing I can do to stop it. I'm not in love with him. I don't have a crush on him. I don't even want him to kiss me, not really, especially not like this. But if I say any of that, it will just look like I'm lying. It's the perfect trap.

Except that for a moment, I actually think he might stand up for me. I actually think he might choose my side. Behind the shock and the mortification, his expression holds the barest hint of delight. But then he looks at the ground and runs his fingers through his hair, sighing deeply. And I know I'm on my own.

The realization hurts more than I thought it would.

"I, uh," he mumbles.

I shake my head and step back as my heart pounds painfully in my chest. "That's not," I stutter. "I mean, I didn't, you know—"

"Just kiss her!" someone shouts.

I freeze.

"Yeah, kiss her, Dean!" another person yells. It's a dare. A joke. A test for Dean at my expense. Will he kiss me for their entertainment? Will he toy with my emotions for them? Pretty soon everyone has joined in the chant. "Kiss her! Kiss her! Kiss her!"

I can't look at him. I can't.

I do. Just one little peek.

He's laughing, as though this is no big deal. And I know if I pretended to be more confident, we could brush the whole incident away. If I were Amanda, I know exactly what I'd do. I'd walk right up to him, kiss him with everything I had, and then I'd walk away, leaving him dazed. I'd come out looking cool, not desperate. I'd come out with the victory.

But I'm not Amanda.

I'm me.

So I stand there frozen, caught in a trap as my embarrassment mounts.

"Kiss her! Kiss her!"

Dean rubs the back of his neck and finally looks at me. He raises his brows as though asking permission, asking if we're in this together. And then he takes a step forward.

I run.

I forget that this was the plan all along. I forget that this is exactly what I was hoping would happen. Tears fall freely down my face as my mortification reaches its peak, and I take off at a sprint, disappearing into the woods.

"Omorose!" Dean calls.

"Let her go," Amanda says loud enough for me to hear.

I don't dare look back.

I keep going until all the hurt is replaced by anger. I'm furious with Amanda for playing me like that. I'm furious at Dean for being able to pretend like it was no big deal. But more than anything else, I'm furious with myself for not being able to do the same.

That was my plan, I try to tell myself. That was exactly what I wanted to happen, what I needed to happen, so I had an excuse to run away.

But deep down, I know the truth. Even if the situation had been different, I still wouldn't have fought back. I would still be here, running away. I'll always be the one with the tear-stained cheeks and not the victorious smile.

The realization consumes me.

My emotions rage, uncontrollably switching from hurt to anger to fear to loathing, a dark spiral without a drop of light. And as I twist further into the chaos, my control over the magic slips away. I try to dig myself out of the bottomless pit, to concentrate on the pounding beat of my feet hitting the ground, but it's a losing battle. I hold on just long enough to break through the line of trees before I trip and fall, tumbling against the grassy plain splayed out before me.

I haven't reached the barrier where the beast's magic obstructs the radar system at the base, but I can't take another step. I can just barely see snow-covered peaks gleaming in the moonlight, and I hope I'm close enough for the beast to reach me before the general does. I hope he senses my magic and recognizes my power for what it truly is—a desperate cry for help.

Before I have time to hope for anything more, my magic takes over.

The torrent carries me away, and I'm drowning in it, sinking to a place I've never gone before. I'm no longer Omorose, no longer a princess, no longer a girl. I am raw energy that has been pent-up for too long. I seep into the ground, strengthening dried out roots, sharpening bent stems, lengthening newborn pines. Flowers sprout to life all around me, fanning out in a circle around my forgotten body. The trees in the distance grow inch by inch as my life force transfers to them, bringing the forest new vigor. I am the sun. My magic is light that nature draws in, and lost as I am, I have no control over how much the greedy, dying world claims. I have no idea how long I lie motionless on the cold ground, power flowing freely into the dirt and the air. I have no awareness. Nothing.

Until finally, the pain comes.

Agony saves me.

I snap back into my body as my soul cries out, begging the magic to stop. I can't move. Every part of me is spent. My muscles ache. Even lifting a finger is too much. But deeper, my chest feels ripped apart, as though each rib was pried away, broken and crunched to pieces, leaving my heart fully exposed. But I hardly feel that ache. It is nothing compared to the torturous pulses that rack through me as time is stripped from my soul. Burning hot and frigid cold waves pass over me, one after the other, over and over as though I am being dipped into two different types of hell. The little rosebud at the center of my being grows smaller as petals fall one by one, disappearing as my life force weakens, dropping away into nothing.

Time is my curse.

Time is being yanked forcibly away.

I'm motionless on the ground as the curse that binds my magic to my soul takes its payment. My vision begins to wane. The already dark world grows darker. Even the moon turns its back on me as silver grows more and more ebony each instant.

Just before I fade entirely, I notice a figure in the distance, the fuzzy outline of a man. Is he friend or foe? I don't know. My eyesight disappears before I find the answer to my question. But it wouldn't matter either way.

I'm in a void, dancing with oblivion.

Yet through the darkness, I feel fingers lightly caress my cheek, as though I am made of stardust, so gentle I fear I'm dreaming. They trace my nose, my chin, up and over my brow, so soft I wonder if it is silk pressing against me. Finally, that phantom touch outlines the edge of my lips, tickling my skin, before it disappears.

I fight to open my eyes.

I fight for one glance.

A warm hand cups the back of my head, pausing for a moment, scorching me with eyes I sense even through the void—eyes that can see every bared part of me, the secret I've kept for so long, the magic I can no longer hide. And then his hold drifts lower down my spine to the curve of my back. Another arm slips beneath my knees, and I'm airborne, being cradled against the night.

All I can think as my consciousness slips away is how infinitely sad it is that I've never felt more precious in my life than I do in this moment, wrapped in the arms of an invisible stranger.

Six

I wake with no sense of time or place. The edges of my memory slip away, a dream I was unable to hold on to. I remember the party. I remember running. I remember my magic. I remember the caress that still burns my skin.

But after that I have nothing.

I'm blank.

My eyes open slowly, and I gasp as I'm blinded by the bright light of day.

The sun.

Warmth seeps into my skin, and I relish in the glow. I'd forgotten how glorious it was just to sit in that radiance, to let the heat wash over me. I've lived in the dark for so long, surrounded only by light that buzzes to life at the flick of a switch. I sit up, basking in the yellow tint blanketing the room.

My eyes go wide as sleep fully fades, and I'm awake enough to take in my surroundings. I'm resting in the center of a four-poster bed, underneath a gauzy canopy, surrounded by gray. But it's not the lifeless color of concrete that I've come to loathe. It's alive, grainy and laced with layers of various shades, the color of rock. I marvel at the sturdy stone walls, the likes of which I have not seen in a decade. A carved wooden armoire fills up the wall to my left, and the other is decorated with a marvelous tapestry, depicting a wolf howling into the moonlight. A bright crackling fire catches my attention, drawing it to the ornate marble fireplace. In those flickering flames, my imagination begins to see something else.

Water springs to my eyes.

I blink it away, but the overwhelming nostalgia remains.

For a moment, I wonder if my sister will run through the door, if this past decade has been a terrible dream. But I don't need to glance down at my mature body to know the truth.

This room looks like home, but it isn't.

There is only one place it can be.

The castle of the beast.

Intrigued, I jump from the bed almost instantly and race to the window, opening it. The world smells wet with morning dew, fresh and vibrant. In the back of my mind, the magic fizzles to life, but after the torrent I released yesterday, there is no yearning pull associated with it. Instead, the magic is there waiting, and I realize I could use it just for fun, just because I want to. But the idea is forgotten as soon as my eyes take in the sprawling town below.

Rows of stone cottages twist and turn in haphazard lines, following winding streets. A crumbling wall encircles the city. And beyond it, everything is white. The land is covered in snow. Tall pine trees are encased in frost. Mountains sweep into the sky. The town is nestled in a quiet valley, and there is nothing but endless wilderness in the distance. I didn't realize how crisp the air was, but now that I have, goose bumps rise along my arms. For the first time, I notice the white cloud forming just beyond my lips as I breathe.

With a shiver, I close the window and let the heat emanating from the fireplace replace the cold I let in. My eyes, however, are still focused outside. I don't realize what I'm looking for until I see it.

Movement.

A furry animal walking on all fours.

A wolf.

And over there, a bear.

My eyes dance from spot to spot, roaming from animal to animal, to the many predators living in peace with one another. Gray wolves, black bears, russet foxes, and even an ivory snow leopard.

I truly am in the realm of the beasts.

And they entrance me.

Is one of them the king? Is one of them my savior from last night? Is one of them the man who touched my face with such affection that my cheeks burn at the memory?

I have to know.

I have to find out.

The jeans and T-shirt I was wearing last night are dirty and rumpled, but they'll do. My arms though are still chilled, and the jacket I had on is nowhere to be seen in this immaculate room. So I open the armoire, smiling when I notice the gowns hanging inside. Velvet trims. Crystal buttons. Pearl adornments. Lace sleeves. Jeweled overlays. I breathe in the beauty filling the closet, too afraid to even touch the fabrics lest they fall apart beneath my unworthy hands. I haven't seen dresses so lovely since my mother was the one wearing them. I never thought I would see anything so perfect again.

But it's too much right now.

A memory I thought I'd forgotten burns to the surface. My mother watching me with her hair twisted and twirled atop her head. Pins rest between her beautiful lips, and her face holds a mix of concentration and love as she takes the small crown from her head and places it atop mine, securing it into place. And then we turn into the mirror, matching in our majesty. My eyes sparkle just like the diamonds decorating the full skirts of my very first big-girl dress.

My mother's face is clearer in that moment than it's been in ten years.

My eyes burn, forcing me to blink the memory away. No matter how hard I try to hold on, the image fades. I'm no longer a little princess with her mother. I'm back to being a lost young woman unsure of her place in the world.

I close the armoire, leaving the gowns untouched.

Maybe another time, but not now. Not yet.

There's a wool blanket resting over a chair by the fireplace, and I take that instead, wrapping it around my shoulders. Not as graceful as the cloak I was searching for, but it's soft and comforting and exactly what I need.

When I reach the door, the knob doesn't turn. At first, I think it's jammed. But the more I twist, the more obvious the truth becomes. It's locked.

A long time ago I loathed being proper.

Then the world changed, and I learned to always follow the rules.

But being in a place that so reminds me of the world I left behind has awakened a little voice I haven't heard in ages.

Go!

My younger self whispers across my mind

Go!

And I want to. I so badly yearn to explore.

So I glance around until I notice a little flowerpot on top of the fireplace. Magic stirs beneath my palms. For the first time, I give in to that light hunger. I use the magic just because I can, not because I'll be ripped apart if I don't. The tingling along my fingertips feels like an old friend I haven't seen in a while. A vine creeps over the edge of the pot, a vine I've brought to life. I urge it on, lending a little piece of myself as the ivy continues to grow and elongate. It twists down the side of the fireplace, over the wall, closer and closer. I focus my attention and push the stalk through the hole of the lock, making it wider and wider until cracks appear in the wood from the strain. An ounce of pain stings my chest, a tiny piece of time being stripped away, but I hardly notice the ache. I'm not using very much magic so the price is not high, and it's easily endured.

When the metal crunches, warping, I pull back on the vine. Listening to me as though alive, it recoils, withdrawing from the lock and attaching to the wall with the rest of the ivy I've just grown. In one quick motion, I halt the flow of magic, controlling it easily, and reach for the knob.

It turns.

I push the door open, allowing a smile to widen my lips, proud when I realize the curve of my lips holds a confident edge. Glowing with life in a way I haven't for years, I make my way down the hall, eager to explore.

I don't run into anyone as I wander. Indeed, the enormous castle is silent. I meander from room to room, running my hands over dusty tapestries, taking note of how many beds look like they haven't been disturbed in years.

Fireplaces are cold. Windows are coated in a thin layer of grime. Even in the bright light of day, the castle is dark. I open curtains as I walk, breathing life back into the stale space, coughing as clouds of dust steal my breath away.

Where is the beast?

Where are his servants?

Why does this place look barren and forgotten?

Why would a king full of magic live in ruin?

The answers don't come as I continue to walk, just more questions.

Every so often, I pause as the ghost of a sound makes its way to my ear, raising the hairs on the back of my neck. The whisper of panting breath. The scuff of paws on stone. The swish of a tail accidently rubbing against the side of a door. Someone is watching me. But when I turn around, no one is there. No animal. No man. Nothing.

The squeak of my sneakers on marble echoes loudly as I make my way down the grand staircase leading to an expansive ballroom. Cobwebs wrap around the chandelier hanging overhead, leaving beautiful metalwork shrouded behind a network of white. The candles look as though they haven't been lit in years. But still, when I see them, another scene comes to mind—a dazzling ballroom sparkling with the light from a hundred quivering candles leaping from mirror to mirror, catching on diamond gowns as they swirled in dance, and sinking into the golden molding decorating every ounce of the room.

I was too young to attend the balls my mother and father used to throw, but my nursemaid usually let me sneak onto the balcony overlooking the ballroom. I would sit there for as long as she would allow, watching the beautiful women in their glittering gowns, wondering when I would get to join them. But my favorite part, the part that now makes my heart ache with longing, was watching my mother and father dance. The world outside of them ceased to exist as the music swelled, and they moved in perfect sync with one another. Their love was tangible, creating a glow just as obvious as the candlelight. I remember smiling as I looked down from my secret spot on the balcony, sitting with my head pressed firmly against the banister, leaning as close as I could, wanting so much to be a part of it.

Before I realize what I'm doing, my eyes are closed, and the world is no longer silent. In my mind, I hear an orchestra playing a hauntingly beautiful melody, a song from somewhere deep inside my soul. My feet move. My body sways. My arms curve. I spin on my toes, dancing, completely carried away by the music and the memories playing on and on in my head.

Laughter shatters the illusion.

I stop abruptly, dropping my arms as my eyes widen, and I turn toward the noise. Breath skipping, I spot a man at the top of the stairs. A scream bubbles up my throat, but I catch it, swallowing it back down as I fight the urge to run.

He is the definition of darkness.

A black cloak drapes over his shoulders, sinking all the way to the floor, blanketing him in ebony. A hood hangs low over his face, covering it in shadows. I can't see any of his features. All I notice is the breadth of his wide shoulders, the sheer size of him.

The beast.

And he is laughing.

At me.

I step back as shame burns my chest. He is a king. And I am just a girl lost in daydreams, dancing with ghosts. I suddenly feel stupid as I stand before him in sneakers and jeans, clutching the wool coverlet around my shoulders as though it is a lifeline, as though it is my shield. I must look like a mess. I never even ran my fingers through my hair, never searched for water to clean my face. I've come here to beg the help of another royal, another magic user thrown into a new world. I came here to be his equal. I should have put on a dress. I should have presented myself in a way befitting my station in life. I should have taken the time to turn myself into the princess I once was, instead of settling for the pauper I've become.

And then I notice he is still laughing.

At me.

At my expense.

And that little girl I heard before comes back.

How dare he mock me!

How dare he!

My anger stirs. She's right. How dare he laugh at me after bringing me to his castle and locking me away with no food, no explanation, no greeting. How dare he sneak around in the shadows, watching me secretly, waiting until my most vulnerable moment to present himself. How dare he mock me when he is the one hiding beneath a layer of fabric, too afraid to show his face.

How dare he!

I brace my feet, straightening my shoulders, standing taller as I face him.

"Princess Omorose Bouchene," I say, surprised at the strength of my voice and how easily the language of my old world rolls off my tongue. And then I curtsy, presenting myself with far more confidence than I feel.

He remains silent, watching me from the shadows of his hood.

The quiet drags. I can't stand it.

"And you are?" I ask, words coming out sharper than I'd intended. But I keep the annoyance burning in my gut, embracing the newfound source of strength.

"I thought you knew," he murmurs, voice rumbling like a storm in the distance, ominous and foreboding.

I swallow, forcing myself to whisper, "The King of Beasts."

He laughs, a wicked, savage thing. The hairs on my arms stand despite the warmth of the blanket draped over my shoulders.

"You sound afraid."

It's not a question.

I wonder if he can smell my fear.

"I'm not," I say, but the words are airy, hardly audible.

The beast relaxes his pose, slouching against the banister and crossing his arms over his chest. The movement causes his sleeves to ride up, and I see his skin for the first time. His forearms are starkly pale against the dark fabric, but my eyes are immediately drawn to the raised, ridged lines crossing over his flesh. He tenses, flexing strong muscles, and I realize they are scars etched like cracks along his porcelain skin. Before I can gawk more, his arms drop back to his sides and he stands swiftly. The sleeves fall back down, masking him in black once more. But the memory lingers.

"Well, you should be afraid, Omorose." He growls my name like wild thunder. "You should be very, very afraid."

I sense movement from the corner of my eye.

I don't want to look. I know it will just feed into whatever this beast has planned for me. But a shiver works its way down my spine, growing stronger as terrified anticipation mounts. I'm not a brave person. Not really. No matter how hard I try. And when the scrape of claws reaches my ear, I jerk my head to the side, searching for the source of the noise as panic clenches my muscles.

Wolves.

A pack of wolves with dark slate fur creeps closer, all eyes trained on me. Predators slowly stalking their prey.

Another sound catches my attention, and I spin to the other side, stomach in my throat. Two giant black bears emerge from the shadows, lips pulled back to show their sharp canines.

I hear another sound, but I don't wait to see what the cause is.

Fear takes over and I run.

The last sound that filters into my ears as I exit the ballroom is his laughter, dark and more dangerous than any of the animals I've left behind.

No one follows.

They let me go. And I recognize the display for what it is, a warning.

It worked.

It's only when I get back to my room, panting and out of breath that I realize I completely forgot about my magic. I was so terrified, so much the coward, I didn't even think to fight back. I ran immediately. I chose fear over strength, as I always do, but this time it hurts more because I could have used my magic, I could have showed him that he didn't scare me.

I still could. But my limbs are shaking, and I don't have the strength to turn around and face him. I barely have the strength to cross the length of the room before collapsing onto my bed

As I curl my knees into my chest, lying on my side, I eye the broken lock on my door. Then my gaze travels to the ivy still wrapped across the wall.

I funnel my magic into those twisting vines and wrap them securely across the entry. Locking the animals out. Locking myself in. Doing the beast's job for him.

Seven

I stay in my room for days, too afraid to face him again, haunted by the idea that my father was right. That I should never have come here. That coming here was the biggest mistake of my life.

Every so often an animal pauses outside my room. The click of paws is unmistakable, as is the low growl. I wait until they've left before cautiously opening the door and retrieving the little bag of food left behind. Usually they give me apples and dried meat. Once there was a loaf of crudely baked bread. I won't complain, not if it means having to leave my room, which I don't. So far, my screaming bladder has been the only source strong enough to force me to leave the sanctuary of these four walls. I found the washroom at the end of the hall on my first day here. The twenty-foot walk to that room is the farthest I'm willing to go, and I don't let my thoughts linger on why there are always fresh buckets of water waiting for me when I need them.

Mostly I lie on the bed, watching the fire or looking over the town below. The only joy I've found since arriving is in finally being able to use my magic freely. The walls of my bedroom have come to resemble a jungle. Ivy vines cover every inch of the stone. Beautiful pink and yellow flowers break up the monotony of green. Today I decided to focus on adding roses to the décor. The deep burgundy buds have just begun to open up. My namesake. But they remind me too much of the dying flower at the center of my soul, marking the toll the magic is taking on my life. So with the flick of my wrist, I change them to white petals, crisp and clean to match the snow just beginning to fall outside the window.

I don't think I'll ever tire of the warm tingle that washes over me whenever my magic is being used. I've become used to the light pain that follows. I hardly feel it anymore. The awe that lifts my heart when I bring life into the world overshadows everything else.

I know I promised my father I would try to get rid of it. But it's my birthright. It's beautiful. It makes me feel like part of my mother is still alive, is still with me. I'm beginning to believe that fifteen short years of having magic, of being able to use it, would be better than a long lifetime without it. But where would I spend those fifteen years? In this room, hiding? I can't live the rest of my life at the base. I can't live it here. I'm not sure there is anywhere in the world that is safe for me when the magic still runs through my veins.

The sound of thudding boots pulls my attention away. With one last glance toward the newly grown ivory petals opening up to welcome the sun, I roll off the bed and walk to the door, pressing my ear against the wood.

The sound of footsteps grows. I furrow my brows, confused. Is it the beast? Is there another human here among us?

The stranger stops before my door. I wait, holding my breath, unable to fight the trickle of fear making its way across my chest.

But then the stomping returns as the man walks away, turns around, walks back, walks away, turns around, walks back.

Is he pacing?

Is he...nervous?

I almost yearn to crack open the door and take a peek. The curiosity itches, taunting me. The stranger stops outside my door once again. The world goes quiet.

"Omorose?"

The low growl washes over me, making me tremble. His voice is too easy to recognize. Even his soft tone is fueled with wild danger. In the back of my mind, I don't see a man on the other side of the door. I see a wolf on the hunt, lazily baring its teeth to a rabbit already caught in its trap.

I'm the rabbit.

"Go away," I plead, voice uneven.

I don't want to talk to the beast. I don't want to see him.

I've been hearing his savage laughter in my dreams. In the nightmare, he is little more than a figure made of shadows, not truly of this world. The thought of him once filled me with hope, but now it makes my blood run cold. Not a beast, but a monster.

"I…" he starts and then trails off, ending with a sigh.

Do I dare say he sounds apologetic? My ears must be deceiving me. I press them closer to the wood, confused.

"Open the door," he commands, anger simmering.

"No," I retort. There's no way I'm opening this door, not for him. I don't want to stare into the shadows of his face, wondering what savage beast hides within the darkness. I'm perfectly fine keeping a wall of wood between us.

"I brought food."

"I don't want it."

"You need to eat."

"No, I don't."

"Omorose," he says gruffly, annoyed.

My stomach rumbles, and I lick my lips. Maybe he does want to help.

Maybe…

"Open the door!" he shouts, slamming his fist into the wood, knocking it into my ear so hard it rings.

I jump away, frightened. "Go away!"

He growls angrily, snarling rather than speaking.

I don't say anything. Neither does he.

We both stay stubborn in our silence.

"Fine, starve," he snaps after a few minutes, finally stomping away.

I fall back against the door, sinking to the floor as my knees slowly give out. I know I've just achieved some sort of victory, but it tastes sour on my tongue. I came here for help. I came here because I thought I might have finally found someone who would understand me. I thought I might have finally found a place where I didn't have to live in fear. What happened to the stranger who caressed my face beneath the moonlight? The person who made me feel for a moment like I wasn't alone? Did I imagine him? There is no doubt in my mind that it couldn't have been this hooded beast with menace seeping from his pores.

I should go home.

I should return to my father.

There is nothing for me here.

But the idea of showing up empty-handed, of going through so much trouble just to see disappointment and despair darken my father's eyes once more, it physically pains me. I'm nauseous just picturing the reunion, just imagining the way his features would fall when I admitted that the miracle he'd been hoping for didn't come true.

But maybe this adventure doesn't have to be for nothing.

Maybe there is something or someone here who will help.

Maybe I don't need the beast. Maybe I just need his books. Or maps. Or scrolls. Anything with any sort of information about the magic. Anything that mentions another person who might be able to help. If I leave, I don't need to go home. Maybe there is another place I can go to seek out acceptance, to finally have a life free of fear.

The idea churns, gaining momentum, gleaming brighter and brighter the more I consider it. Before I realize what I'm doing, magic pricks my fingertips as the vines are swept away from the door. I throw on the cloak I found in the armoire and slip into my sneakers before stepping into the empty hallway. Then I close my eyes, using the magic to extend my senses, hoping it will guide me toward answers.

At first, I feel nothing aside from the usual pulse of nature.

And then I feel it.

A gentle tug on the edge of my magic, as though someone is tenderly urging me closer. I'm not afraid. I know there is no way the beast could be the source of that supernatural caress. I haven't felt his magic, but I don't need to. His power would be a tornado pulling me in, sweeping me up, overpowering me, wild and untamed. But the magic calling out to me now is the epitome of delicate control.

Hope swells.

I grin.

Without hesitating, I follow the path the magic has laid out. Each step feels like it's in the right direction. Maybe I was supposed to come here after all. Maybe the fear was worth it.

I march through the halls, not pausing to look at the rooms filtering by. Bedrooms and sitting rooms merge together, until I'm led to a central staircase I never noticed the last time I decided to explore. I take the steps two at a time, crossing over into a wing of the giant castle that I haven't been to before.

The halls are dark.

A forbidden aura permeates the air.

I continue following the tug on my magic, trying not to notice how the eyes on the tapestries feel as though they're following me. Heat tickles the back of my neck, as though my own body is warning me not to walk any closer.

But the lure of that foreign magic grows stronger each second, grows more enticing. I have to know what it is. I have to know if it can help me. So against all my instincts, I keep going. I don't stop until I see a faint golden glow seeping through the crack beneath a door at the end of a hallway. And then I'm sprinting as excitement punches through me.

When I reach it, I rip the door open, searching for the source of the magic. I don't need to search for very long. My eyes are immediately drawn to a glowing woman resting peacefully on the bed.

"Hello?" I whisper, too amazed to really speak.

She doesn't respond. Doesn't stir. Doesn't give any indication that she's heard me. But the aura surrounding her brightens as though thrilled. The foreign magic that had been tugging me closer grows warm and encouraging.

I take a step toward her.

And another, crossing the room until I am standing over her motionless body, looking down upon the most beautiful face I've ever seen. Despite the darkness of the room, her skin holds a perfect summer tan. Honey-colored hair gleams against the pillows, creating a path my eye follows to the long and lean arms crossed over her chest. Her face holds a pixie shape, narrow with high-defined cheekbones and pink lips that look shiny with gloss. I couldn't guess how old she is even if I tried. A translucent film encases her entire body, and for a moment I think there are wrinkles around the corners of her closed eyes, but a second later they disappear. The golden light filling the room radiates from within her, as though she is a star that has fallen down to Earth.

I'm mesmerized.

My fingers reach for her skin, to feel if she's real. Surely someone so perfect can't truly exist.

What is her magic?

Who is she?

Why is she here?

And more importantly, why did she lead me to her?

"Don't move another inch."

The snarl catches me off-guard. My heart leaps into my throat as I snatch my hand away and turn around all in one quick motion.

The beast is watching from the doorway, wearing the same midnight cloak from the day before. But with the golden glow filling the room, I can just see the bottom edge of his lip and the strong curve of his masculine chin. For some reason, the sight comforts more than scares me. He's a man, after all. His face is a normal face. But in my mind, I still imagine his eyes are red and glowing, feral. The gaze I cannot see shifts, and he turns his head slightly to the side. But it's enough for me to notice the edge of a faint scar marring the otherwise unblemished ivory skin to the left of his lips.

He takes a step closer. Too close.

He towers over me, at least a foot taller and maybe twice as wide. I've never felt so small, so frail, in my entire life.

"What are you doing in here?" he growls deeply, simmering with anger.

I keep my shoulders straight, rigid. I'm done cowering before him. "I was tired of sitting in my room. I needed to get out for a little while."

He snorts. "That's funny. When I stopped by this morning, you seemed perfectly content to stay in there forever."

"Of course I did, when the other option was going anywhere with you." The retort rolls off my lips with surprising ease. I clench my jaw to keep it from dropping.

The muscles around the beast's jaw clench too, but his hands tighten into fists, covering unspoken rage.

A satisfied feeling settles over me. I got to him. Take that.

The feeling dissipates a moment later when he leans intimidatingly forward, making the space between us taut and tense. "What are you doing in here?"

I take a step back, looking over my shoulder at the woman. "I felt the magic. I just wanted to see where it was coming from."

He inhales sharply. "Don't go any closer."

I focus my attention back into the shadows shrouding his face. "Who is she?"

"None of your business."

"She's beautiful," I murmur, wondering if she's special to him, if a beast is capable of love.

"I said, none of your business. Now step away."

But I don't want to step away. Something about her magic is magnetic, pulling for me, as though I've slipped into a spinning vortex and there's no choice but to get sucked inside.

My fingers reach back, pressing against the bed. So close.

"Stop!" he barks. "I won't tell you again."

But I feel outside of myself, as though I have no control over my movements. My mind grows fuzzy and disjointed the farther back my fingers slide. Magic sizzles on my skin, my magic yearning to connect with hers. My arm continues to stretch toward her while my gaze stays on the beast. He's trembling as though his body is fighting with his mind for control. I wonder if I should feel afraid. But my emotions are so far away. My mind is distant. My whole body bends back toward the woman, until...

We connect.

My eyes go wide as the gentle pull on my magic becomes a furious yank, and my whole body jerks toward her, throwing me off-balance as I tumble over, landing on the bed. My magic leeches into her, and I'm so utterly confused, I can't catch up with what's happening. My magic doesn't affect people. I can't heal a dying woman. The only thing I can give life to is plants. So why is she absorbing my power like a tree in the desert, thirsty with starvation?

My gaze shifts to the beast.

Does he feel it?

Does he know what it means?

But when my eyes land upon him, he is not a man anymore. The body beneath the cloak is rippling, expanding, growing higher and larger. The pale color of his hands is darkening as his nails elongate and fur pushes through translucent skin. His fingers change shape. His body bends over, landing on all fours against the floor. And suddenly, in the blink of an eye, the cloak covering him disappears and a snarling black bear stands before me, revealing sharp canines. He roars, rearing up on hind legs and slashing jagged claws toward my face.

I scream.

A high-pitched, terrified sound.

The horror is enough of a distraction that I forget about the woman and the magic and the questions I was about to ask. I forget my vow not to hide anymore. I forget my promise to be brave. I forget everything.

All I know is the door is open, and in the time it takes for the beast to release another bloodcurdling roar, I'm already sprinting through it.

Eight

I'm blinded by fear as I race through the castle halls. All I can think is, go! Get away! Run! Quickly!

So I do.

Across the halls. Down the staircase. Through the front door.

I'm outside before I even realize it, racing down the front steps of the castle and diving into the main stretch of the town. I've gazed at these streets from above for the past few days, so I know if I follow this road it will lead me to a gate, it will lead me away. And that's where I have to go. Away. Home. To another city. Anywhere but here in this castle with that monster.

My eyes stay straight ahead. I don't allow them to focus on the wolves and bears watching me as I dash by. The animals become little more than dark shadows in my peripheral. My vision tunnels on the open iron gate just visible at the end of the street. And once I'm through it, my world is washed in white. Snow covers every inch of the land. I pass by icy trees as my feet sink deeper with each step. My breath grows short as my muscles scream at me with exertion. But I don't stop. The mountains begin to incline, but still I keep going.

Then I trip on a rock.

I fall, landing wrists first against the ground. Frost stings my exposed skin and a deep freeze sinks into my bones when the snow wraps around me. As the adrenaline leaves my system, the sweat on my arms brings a chill to my muscles. The silent forest is filled with the clatter of my shivering teeth and the puff of my breath as I blow warm air into my palms. Only then do I realize how cold it is. How lost I am. And how low the sun has begun to hang in the sky.

Only then do I realize my mistake.

I turn, but there is nothing but ivory stretching out in every direction. The gently falling snow has begun to pick up. I could follow my footsteps back toward the castle, but I'm not sure if it would be any safer there or if I should take my chances with the wilderness. More so, I'm almost certain my fatigued body would give out before I made it back.

Survival instincts take over. Magic burns to life in my chest, providing some warmth, but not enough. I focus on the ground below me, forcing flowers to grow through the frozen soil, willing them to lift higher and spread wider until the space beneath my feet is cleared of snow and replaced with a small patch of color. Still shivering, I sit and wrap the cloak tightly around me. It's warm, but not warm enough to keep the wintry breeze out. So I concentrate on something that might. Bushes spring to life, surrounding me like a wall against the chill. I twist and turn the branches until they meet overhead, blocking out the light but also the wind, leaving me in shadows. Then I hug my knees to my chest, trying to use my breath to keep my frigid body warm.

For a while, I think it might work.

Then the wind picks up.

The flurries turn to icy pellets.

Freezing water drips through the cracks in the bushes, soaking into my clothes.

In what little light I have, I notice my fingertips are turning a dangerously pale shade, and I've begun to lose feeling. When I press my hand to my nose, the tip feels like ice. Just when I'm about to shift the plants away, to admit defeat and try to find my way back to the castle, a thunderous voice stops me.

"Omorose!"

It's him. He followed me. I hug my knees closer to my chest, as if to hide myself more.

"I don't want to hurt you!" he shouts. "I'm." He pauses. "I'm sorry. Please, you have to come with me." His voice is getting louder. He's coming closer. "You'll die out here. On a night like this, you'll never survive."

I know he's telling the truth.

But I can't fight the fear churning in my gut. It overwhelms me. And when I close my eyes, I don't see a man calling my name. I see a monstrous bear with saliva falling from gleaming teeth. I see my doom.

"Omorose?"

This time it is little more than a whisper. He's right next to my hideout. I can hear him breathing. My fingers tremble. Snow crunches as he steps in a circle around me. I'm caught. I'm trapped.

Then I hear that little girl again.

Fight! she whispers in the back of my mind. *Fight back!*

And I remember that I'm strong.

I'm powerful.

And I don't want to run away any longer.

My magic acts on reflex. One moment I am cowering. And the next, the bushes around me have recoiled and vines are ripping free of the ground, soaring toward the beast, sharp with thorns. He leaps away, quick on his feet. The hood of his cloak falls, but with his back turned to me, I only notice jet-black hair before I sink deeper into the magic, too wrapped up in the power to notice anything else. I am one with those prickly branches lashing out at the beast. More rise from the ground, sprouting from everywhere at once, surrounding him like a spiky cell. They sink closer, shrinking around his form until sharp edges press against his skin.

Have I caught the beast?

But a howl blasts through the air, loud enough that it seems to vibrate over the mountains. As the sound stretches, it turns into a furious roar. The black cloak ripples, warping and changing, until the same bear from before bursts to life. Claws slash, ripping the vines apart. Thick branches snap like little more than twigs. In seconds, my trap is shredded apart.

Then the bear turns toward me.

Breath smokes from his flared nostrils. Deep, gray eyes barrel down on me, storm clouds churning, dark and dangerous.

He takes a step forward.

I stumble back.

My chest begins to hurt as the cost of my magic slowly takes its toll. Waves of fire and ice roll through me as my life is methodically stripped away by the curse. But I keep the magic burning. I bite back the pain.

Vines break through snow, stretching into the sky.

The beast wipes them away easily.

But I keep throwing them at him. It's the only thing I can think of. My magic is supposed to be beautiful and gentle. It's not made for battle. But he is. Everything about him screams weapon. Blood drips from his limbs and paws as thorns carve into his flesh. Bright red droplets stain the snow. But he continues moving forward, unrelenting.

I know the exact moment he tires of this game. A low growl rumbles from deep in his chest. He pauses for just an instant. Then he leaps across the space between us, opening his jaws wide, as though to swallow me whole.

Magic surges through me.

A pine tree erupts from the ground, exploding into the world like a bomb as snow and dirt are sent flying. In less than a second, it stretches fifty feet high, trunk growing thicker and thicker. Time slows. I fall back on the ground, strength depleted.

A deafening crack fills the air.

The beast slams into the tree at full force, shattering the sturdy wood. The ground shakes when his heavy form drops down.

Then silence.

Long, lingering silence.

I stand cautiously, peering through the falling snow toward the unmoving body on the ground.

Is he dead?

Did I kill him?

The idea provides no comfort. Instead, anxiety racks through me. My lips quiver and my head begins to shake back and forth with denial. I meant to stop him. I meant to show him I could fight back, that I was strong too. I never meant to…to kill him.

Did I?

I bite my lip as my heart skips a beat.

Am I a murderer?

"No!" I gasp.

And then I'm running across the small space, falling on my knees beside his motionless limbs. The bear is gone. And with the cloak pulled away, I finally see the beast for who he really is instead of the creature my fear turned him into.

Not a monster.

Not a king.

A man.

Young, just like me.

I drop my ear to his chest, listening desperately, sighing when I hear the gentle thump of his heartbeat.

Not dead.

Knocked out, but not dead. At least not yet.

Relief floods through me. I'm not a killer. Not a monster. And looking down at him, I'm beginning to wonder if maybe the beast isn't either. With eyes closed in sleep, he looks so gentle and innocent. Before I realize what I'm doing, my palm reaches down to cup his cheek. His skin is soft. The heat of it warms my frigid fingers. But it's not smooth. His face is laced with delicate scars, some deeper than others. But he is so pale the lines are almost translucent. Except for three severe cuts on either side of his forehead, healed-over gashes slicing deeply through his temples. They're nearly symmetrical, cutting into his hairline just above both of his ears. My fingers drift up, tracing his mutilated skin, before drifting higher to run through his coarse onyx hair. It feels like velvety fur.

A soft purr distracts me.

I look over my shoulder into a set of bright golden eyes. They look human. They look woefully concerned. But it's the body of a snow leopard that slinks toward me, nearly camouflaged by the falling snow. For the first time, I'm not afraid. Its thick paw nudges the beast, but he doesn't stir.

"He's alive," I assure the animal.

Those golden eyes find mine again, filled with understanding—far more understanding than any animal's should be. But before I have time to process, howls reach my ears, mournful cries that pierce the air and echo toward me. Over my shoulder, gray shadows appear in the distance, growing larger and more distinct, until a pack of wolves emerges from the shadows, running closer. They don't stop until they surround us, all eyes on the beast.

An undeniable sense of love permeates the space.

I'm the outsider once again.

But more than that, I'm the cause of all their worry.

"I'm sorry," I whisper. "I'm so very sorry. He frightened me. I got scared, and I just acted out of instinct. I didn't mean…"

They're wild animals, but they don't lash out for vengeance, they don't let their gut reactions control them. In fact, they hardly notice me.

The lead wolf steps beside me, nuzzling the beast's neck, so close I could reach out and pet the fluffy white fur on the underside of its belly. Steam escapes its parted lips as the wolf licks the beast's cheek, trying to wake him. It whines a sad, screechy sound when the beast doesn't move. And then it looks over its shoulder to the rest of the pack. Without needing to speak, they march forward, determined. While the leader watches, the rest of the wolves dig into the snow, deep enough so they can crawl beneath the beast's body. They wriggle under, matting their coats with dirt and frost, and then stand with his heavy weight stretched across them. His hands fall to either side, leaving his fingertips to brush against the ice while they walk away. I follow the red traces of blood dripping from his skin, unable to look away.

When they disappear into the depths of the storm, I finally remember how cold I am. My skin trembles. But I can't move. I stare into the emptiness, utterly torn, remembering the beast's last words to me.

I don't want to hurt you.

On a night like this, you'll never survive.

I was too blinded by fear to realize it, but he was out here to save me. To bring me back to the warmth of the castle, not to hunt me down and hurt me. Only after I attacked did he unleash the beast within.

But before, the way he laughed so harshly at my silent dance.

The way he slammed his fist into my door when I wouldn't let him in.

The way he attacked me for touching that glowing woman.

No, I don't trust him.

But, I realize confidently, I no longer fear him.

And I can't ignore the fact that I'm intrigued. By him. By the mysteries of his kingdom. By the whisper in the back of my mind telling me that maybe it was the beast who found me in that field a few days ago, who held me in his strong, sturdy arms, whose touch whispered that I'd finally found a place I might belong.

A soft downy head presses into my palm, and I realize I had forgotten about the leopard with the golden eyes. It nudges my leg, but I don't understand. It nudges again. But I don't move. Then it growls, looking up at me with a hint of frustration, and starts to walk away.

I try to follow, but my feet are frozen. My body has no strength. The shivers grow unbearable. And with nothing to distract me, the weariness mounts. Between the escape, the cold, the storm, the battle, and the toll of my magic, my body shuts down. I slink slowly toward the ground, utterly fatigued.

In one leap, the giant cat is beneath me, catching me before I fall. I'm not very large or very heavy, so it waits patiently for me to crawl onto its back before carrying me away. I breathe in the warmth of its fur, letting the heat of its body course through me. And together we travel through the storm.

Nine

I must have passed out during the journey home, because when I wake, I am curled against the leopard's side, resting before the fire in my room in the castle. Two large golden eyes watch me curiously as I sit up.

My whole body aches.

Every inch of me yearns for a hot bath. For warm food. For more sleep.

But when I open my mouth, unexpected words pop out. "Where is he?"

The leopard yawns, stretching its jaws fully wide while its tongue extends out. I catch a quick glance of sharp canines. And then it shakes its head and rolls smoothly to its feet, pausing for a moment to kneel down in a long back-extending stretch.

Envying its feline grace, I push awkwardly to my feet, wincing as my muscles scream that I should not be standing, should not be moving.

As the leopard struts out the door, not waiting for me to follow, I eye the armoire wistfully. But there's no time for me to try on dresses, to find one that might hopefully fit. My impatience wins out. The last time I saw the beast he was barely breathing, and I won't be calm until I know he's awake.

Quickly, I grab the wool blanket resting on the chair and wrap it comfortably around my shoulders. Let the beast laugh at my funny outfit again if he wants. The more he's laughing, the more he'll hopefully forget that I almost killed him.

I enter the hallway just in time to see an ivory tail disappear around the corner and I hurry to follow. The leopard leads me through familiar corridors, to the central staircase I first made my way up the day before. When we reach this far wing of the castle, the halls still hum with an ominous, foreboding sort of air. The curtains are all closed, cloaking the space in shadows. But we turn down new corridors. I don't see the glowing door or the beautiful woman slumbering behind it. We walk farther and farther, to what I can only imagine is the complete other end of the castle, and then we stop beside a closed door. The leopard leans onto its hind legs, reaching a paw up to turn the knob. And from the light shining through a narrow crack in the curtains, I see the beast.

His eyes are still closed.

My heart sinks.

The pack of wolves from yesterday lie scattered across the floor, and I step between them to the windows, throwing the curtains wide.

They all whine, growling softly.

"Hush!" I order, then pause.

When did I become confident enough to chide wolves?

But they remain quiet, listening to me, so I bolster the newfound assurance and give them each a pointed stare as I continue to adjust the rest of the curtains, not stopping until the entire room is bathed in sunlight.

Finally able to see clearly, I glance around, realizing something. The beast is a total mess. A slob, I mean. Clothes lay in disarray all over the place. Chairs are knocked over on their sides. Pillows rest scattered across the floor. The only thing in the entire room that seems to be in its perfect spot is a painting hanging over the fireplace, a young boy with his parents. A young boy with ebony hair, ivory skin, and eyes the color of a rainstorm.

Before I can take a closer look, a soft moan draws my attention to the bed.

The beast is wriggling in his skin, showing signs of life. But his eyes are still closed. I put a hand to his brow. It feels warm. But he's not sweating or mumbling. He doesn't seem feverish. Yet he flinches in his sleep, shaking his head, almost as though in the middle of a terrible dream.

"Shh."

I lift myself beside him on the soft mattress, leaning over to stroke the line of his cheekbones until the creases leave his face. He leans into my palm as though sensing my touch, as though it pulls him from the nightmare. He sighs and a small smile settles onto his lips.

My heart twinges tenderly.

I'm so startled by the reaction that I pull away.

But not far.

My eyes continue to roam, and it's only then that I notice the angry scratches covering his arms and the gashes along his fingertips. Painful cuts from the extra sharp thorns I used to attack him. They're still red and raw.

I turn to the wolves, knowing they'll somehow understand me. "I need a bowl and a rock. Water if you can find it. Fresh towels. And most importantly, a potted plant. A flower. Anything with soil. It doesn't matter."

They leave quickly, returning one by one with all the items I need, dropping them at my feet. The lessons my mother taught me a decade ago come flooding back. Magic burns my fingertips as I breathe medicinal herbs to life, the kind my mother showed me how to use to help heal wounds. Using the rock, I crush the leaves against the side of the bowl, adding water and a little dirt, until I have a dark evergreen salve.

The work is easy and comes naturally to me. After all, this is the beauty my magic was created for, to give life, to save it. Not to end it. Using the towel, I wash the cuts clean and cake the mud all over the beast's exposed skin, trying not to focus on the fact that he's not wearing a shirt...and might not be wearing any clothes for that matter.

My cheeks burn at the thought.

I can't stop the blush as it comes.

But I could stop looking. I could give myself more breathing room.

I don't.

If anything, I grow more and more intrigued. Scars decorate his skin like tattoos, various shapes and shades. Some are deep and dark. Others are pale and only brush over the surface. The marks of different sets of claws, a strange sort of artwork. But the more I look, the more I touch, and the more I can't help but notice how sturdy the muscles beneath those scars are. My fingers trace the curve of his hard bicep, the slope of his wide shoulder, the strong edge of his masculine jaw. The only part of him that looks soft is his lips.

"Enjoying the view?"

It takes a second for the words to register. And another for me to realize they came from the plush mouth I'd just been admiring.

I snap up.

I'm staring into tumultuous clouds, about to get swept away in the dark storm churning in his eyes. Or maybe I'm already there.

"You can stop," he growls, narrowing his gaze.

He tries to sit up, but I press on his shoulders. "Stay put," I demand. And it takes every ounce of my strength to keep him down. "I'm trying to help you."

His nostrils flare. "Why?"

"Relax, okay?" I mumble. For some reason, it's become easy for me to boss him around. "You never would have gotten these cuts yesterday if you hadn't followed me into the storm. If you hadn't come to save me."

He lifts his brows, eyeing me pointedly. "I think you mean I never would have gotten these cuts if you hadn't tried to kill me."

I swallow, dropping my gaze, and then shrug, getting back to the work of rubbing the salve over his wounds. I'm very conscious of putting my fingers on the green mud and only the green mud, keeping the urge to let my hands wander in check. "That's beside the point."

"You're right," he says and reaches out to grasp my arms, halting my movements. Without meaning to, my gaze finds his again. "The point is I'm fine. As you've no doubt noticed, it's not the first time I've been injured, and it definitely won't be the last."

"Well," I say, drawing the word out as I try to whip my arms out of his hold. But his grip is a vice I can't shake. The more I try, the more futile I realize it is. Huffing, I look back to him, annoyed by the smirk that's suddenly sprouted to life on his lips. There's something about him that just makes me want to wipe that grin right off his face.

Something that makes me want to fight rather than back down. Something that pushes all of my normal wallflower urges to the far corners of my mind. "This is the first time you've been injured by me. So will you just let go of me and let me help?"

"No," he says smoothly, still smiling.

And before I know what's happening, his hold shifts to my waist as he sits up and easily places me back on the ground. By the time I blink, he's already rolled off the bed to a standing position, moving with all the stealth of a silent predator.

"You should really lie down," I murmur.

He just glares at me.

But a moment later, my point is proven when he takes two wobbly, uneven steps. His eyes go wide and he rapidly blinks, and I know all the blood is rushing toward his head, stealing his sight. By the time I dive to catch him, he's already on the ground.

The wolves start barking.

For a moment, my breath catches as a little trickle of fear stirs in the back of my mind. But when I meet their angry eyes, I realize the wolves aren't mad at me. They're mad at him.

The beast bares his teeth, pulling his lips back, emitting a low growl. Though he still looks like a man, down on all fours with that deep rumble, he seems more animal than human. The pack leader who licked his face with such concern the night before steps forward and snarls harshly. All the wolves creep closer, surrounding him, jaws open.

The beast watches them all. Then he relaxes, rolling his eyes, and is back in bed in a heartbeat.

"You can finish whatever you were doing," he drawls, holding out the bowl of green salve to me. "It seems I'm outnumbered."

And when he says that last part, he glances at the pack leader with a wry brow raise. The wolf promptly releases an apologetic whine and leaps onto the bed, curling into the beast's side. He raises his brows at the animal, but the wolf responds by opening its mouth wide and letting its tongue roll to the side. I almost think it's smiling. And then the beast grins, reaching a hand out to scratch between the wolf's ears.

Hesitantly, I reach for the bowl the beast is holding out for me, careful not to touch his fingers. This time, I don't kneel over him on the bed. I remain on my feet, keeping a little more distance.

"They seem concerned about you," I mutter, trying to understand the interactions I've been witnessing.

"They are," he replies offhandedly.

"Why?"

He flicks his eyes toward me quickly and then looks away, but not before I see into the haunted depths of his smoky irises. He keeps his focus on the wolf as he softly replies, "Because I'm their king."

He doesn't say anymore. And I can tell from the softly whispered tone not to press any further. The beast has secrets. So do I. So does everyone.

Instead, I focus on my work, dipping my fingers into the healing mud and spreading it over the angry red cuts covering his skin. But the more I touch him, the more aware I am of the intimacy of the situation. My skin on his skin. The heat that starts to fill the air. How our breath mingles in the somewhat small space between us. And the more I try to take my mind off the beast and focus on the salve, the more awkward I become. My fingers begin to shake nervously.

"What's your name?" I ask suddenly, a little too loudly. I meant to sound absently curious, but I don't think it came out that way. Swallowing, I keep my gaze focused intensely on my fingers, not giving in to the urge to take a quick glance at the beast.

I'm desperate for a distraction.

"Cole," he murmurs, voice vibrating with the purr of a jungle cat.

For some reason, the sound of it sends a delightful shiver down my spine. *Stay focused*, I try to tell myself. Still, I can't help it when his name rolls off my tongue.

"Cole," I repeat quietly. Something about saying it out loud seems dangerous, like I'm breaking a rule. His name holds that same delicious wildness that buzzes beneath his skin.

I shake my head a little.

When did that wildness become delicious? Not scary or fearful or terrifying, but delicious?

"Why'd you come here, Omorose?" he asks.

I don't respond right away. My fingers have found their way to the bottom of his arm, to the strong hand coiled into a fist. One by one, I unlatch his fingers, forcing my breath to remain even as I examine his palm, noticing that it takes both of my hands just to hold one of his. I know somewhere underneath his skin there are claws and fur, but right now, all I see are callouses and scratches that are utterly human.

As I hold his hand, gently applying the salve, I find myself telling him my story, telling him the truth, a truth I've never told anyone in my entire life. "I came from your world," I begin. "My parents were the King and Queen of Roanoe. People used to call our kingdom the most beautiful in the world, and it was. Gardens lined each street. Every day was like spring, warm with the promise of new life. Our people were happy and loyal and had everything they would ever need. And I did too. My mother, my father, my sister. And then everything changed. On the day of the earthquake, I was traveling with my father to visit another ruling family, and when the ground finally settled we found ourselves at the entrance to another world. People grabbed us, stole everything we had and locked us away. My father agreed to give them information in exchange for our safety, and we've been living with the people of Earth ever since."

"But why are you here?" he urges gently.

I grip his hand tighter, not realizing that I've stopped applying the salve and am just holding on to him now, like a lifeline. "Something else happened on the day of the earthquake. I got my magic. My mother died. My sister died. Everyone we've ever known vanished when the worlds merged, our kingdom, our home, and our loved ones. My father and I were alone in a new world, a world where magic was seen as evil. I had to hide. I was afraid of discovery every day for a decade. And then, my...well, I learned that someone dear to me had died, that the people of Earth murdered him because of his magic, and I knew I had to leave. I knew I couldn't hide any longer. So I came here."

I finally look up.

His gray eyes stare intensely at me, seeing all the way into my soul. But I can't read the dark and mysterious emotions swirling within them.

"Your magic called out to me," I continue, pressing forward. "I thought if I came, I might finally find people who understand me, who understand my magic, who realize its beauty. I thought if I came, I might finally find a place I belong."

I lick my lips, sealing them, waiting.

We watch each other.

I know my words contain unspoken questions.

Is this a place where I might belong?

Is he someone who might finally understand me?

I don't realize I'm holding my breath until my chest begins to ache. But I'm afraid that any movement will break this drawn-out moment, will let the beast get away without answering. And I need an answer.

"Please go."

The words are so muted I almost don't hear them.

Cole blinks, ripping his hand away, and the illusion shatters.

He doesn't care about me.

He's a beast.

And he always will be.

"Get out," he growls harshly.

I flinch back, eyes burning at the rejection after baring my secrets so freely.

"Get out!" he roars.

I do.

Not because he told me to. Not because of the menacing thunder in his voice. Not because of the fear crawling back out from the corner of my mind. None of those reasons, though they all play a part.

I leave because of my pride, what little of it I have left after an entire life of pretending and hiding. I leave because he's seen me terrified and lonely and afraid. I leave because he's seen me vulnerable and weak. I leave because he's seen all of those things, but there's one thing he hasn't.

I leave because I won't let him see me cry.

Ten

I spend the rest of the day sitting on the windowsill in my bedroom, staring at the snow-covered town below. Then I go to sleep. And when I wake up, I find myself back on that perch, looking out into the mountains, trapped by my own indecision.

For a moment, I really thought I could see myself here. For a moment, I truly believed Cole would accept me, would tell me I could stay.

But now I don't know what to believe.

He was so cruel. He's been so cruel.

But he chased after me in the storm. He must have been the one who brought me here after I ran away from the base. I haven't seen another human anywhere.

And why is that?

Why is Cole the only one with a human form?

And who was that glowing woman?

Why didn't Cole want me to go near her?

I should probably leave. I'm not wanted. But I'm not even sure where I am or how to go away.

How long did it take Cole to bring me here? After that splurge of magic, I could have been unconscious for a few hours, a day, maybe two, maybe a week. Even with the right supplies, could I make it through the mountains on my own?

"Omorose?"

I turn, gasping with shock as the sound of my name interrupts my thoughts.

Cole stands in my doorway with his arms crossed, leaning casually against one side. I can't help but notice the ebony cloak is gone, replaced with pants, boots, and a white long-sleeve shirt slightly open at the collar. More casual, maybe. More handsome, definitely. But he still emits an air of danger I can't ignore. One that makes my pulse race. But I can't quite tell if the thud of my heart is from excitement or alarm, the lines are a little too blurred.

"Did I frighten you?" he asks innocently.

"Which time?" I retort. He has the decency to look chagrined. Yet that look just spikes my frustration. He should be embarrassed and ashamed. He knew exactly what he was doing. "But wasn't that the point?" I accuse. There's a fire in my voice that I don't usually hear. Acidity too. "I believe your exact words the first time we met were, 'You should be afraid, Omorose. You should be very, very afraid.' Well, your message was received loud and clear."

He shifts his weight, reaching one arm up to rub the back of his neck. Finally, he's the one who's uncomfortable.

"I don't want you to be afraid," he says with a sigh, looking at me from beneath hooded brows. "Not anymore."

"Why did you?" I'm not letting him off that easy.

"I didn't trust you."

"And now?"

"I still don't."

I gape at him. "That makes no sense."

"Maybe not." He shrugs. "But who said I have to make sense?"

"Me," I say, totally agitated. "I do. And I need a better explanation than that if I'm going to stay here a second longer. Otherwise, I'll take my chances on the mountains."

He growls under his breath, not looking the least bit apologetic anymore. But I cross my arms and stand my ground, not backing down. He doesn't scare me, not anymore.

"Look," he snaps. And then he pauses, taking a deep breath while he unclenches his fists. "Look," he repeats, softer this time. "I can't tell you anything, not yet anyway. There are a lot of reasons why, a lot of people who depend on me, but the biggest reason I can't explain anymore is because I don't trust you, not yet. But I want you to stay. I want you to be at ease in my home. And I want those things because I don't trust you, but there's a part of me that thinks maybe someday I could."

I take a deep breath. His words affect me more than I realized they would, more than he knows. I repeat quietly, "You want me to stay?" He wants me, someone wants me—the real me.

The gray in his eyes softens, less like a storm and more like the downy fur of the wolves. Irresistible. "Yes, I want you to stay." His Adam's apple bobs as he swallows and looks down to the floor, then back up at me. "I have a feeling we could both use a friend."

His gaze ensnares me. "Friends?"

He smiles hesitantly, as though his cheek is tugging forcefully on his lip to move it just the least bit upward, as though his face isn't used to the motion. "Yeah, friends."

"Well, friends apologize," I murmur, words spilling out before I've fully processed them. But they're the truth. I can't be a friend to someone who intentionally set out to terrify me, not unless he apologizes first.

"I'm sorry," he replies immediately.

But I just stare at him unsatisfied. Remorse shouldn't be quick and easy. It demands an explanation or it's not real. So I keep looking at him, silently watching as he shifts his weight from the doorway to stand straight. His eyes flick all around the room, landing on everything except for me. Tension oozes from his frame, uncomfortable stiffness. Until finally, everything about him releases all at once.

"Okay," he mutters, "I'm sorry. I'm sorry for frightening you. I'm sorry for the way I introduced myself.

I'm sorry for snapping at you. I'm sorry for making you so terrified that you thought you needed to run away. I'm sorry for what happened right before you ran, for, well, shifting in front of you. And, most of all, I'm sorry for shouting at you yesterday. I didn't realize how hard it was for you to tell me your story until I watched you run away, until I thought about how difficult it would be to tell you mine."

I lick my lips. There's one more thing he did, something I'm not even sure he remembers doing. "Are you sorry for laughing at me?" I ask.

His brows furrow as though he doesn't know what I'm talking about. And then they widen almost imperceptibly. He steps closer, but then stops himself, shifting his head to peer at me thoughtfully. "Yes," he answers, and his voice truly sounds regretful. "I'm sorry for laughing at you."

My lips twitch into a smile for a second, but I push it away with a shrug. "All right, then I'll be your friend."

I extend my arm, offering to shake on it. He walks close enough to entwine his palm with mine. I forgot how large his hands were, how large he was. But as I turn up to look into his face, which towers a foot above mine, I realize he is already gazing down at me, watching as though realizing for the first time how small I am. The thought makes me want to laugh. I grin instead. But the change in my expression makes his eyes darken a smidge.

We don't shake.

We stand there staring at one another, stuck on either side of an invisible line.

"The magic," he says gruffly, voice more aggressive than I think he means it to be, as though the mere topic causes a surge in his anger. "If we're going to be friends, can you promise me one thing? We won't talk about it, won't discuss it. You won't ask questions about it or even bring it up. No magic, nothing at all. Can you do that? At least until I change my mind?"

No. The word rushes to my lips, but I manage to hold it back, to keep it inside. No. I don't want to make that promise. The whole reason I came was to learn about magic, to meet another person who has magic, to share that part of myself with someone. The whole reason I came was so I wouldn't have to hide any longer.

But I swallow my protests back down.

For now, I can make that promise.

For now, we can be friends, and I can give him the time he needs to trust me. I can take that time to learn to trust him.

For now, I can keep my magic to myself.

"Okay," I say, voice strong.

He smiles then, wide and welcoming, and it makes his entire face light up. All the hard, harsh lines wash away, leaving someone I hardly recognize behind.

Slowly, our hands pulse up and down twice.

The deal is done.

But I can't help but notice how he lingers for one little moment, touching me longer than necessary before he pulls his hand gently away. I can't help but notice how my fingers stretch for him, how cold my skin feels without his warmth seeping into it.

"Come on," he says, nudging his head toward the door and asking me to follow. "You shared some of your story with me, I figure it's my turn to return the favor. Unless, of course, you just enjoy being locked in here by yourself all day."

"What did you have in mind?" I ask, picking up his playful tone and using one of my own.

"You'll see," he replies mysteriously and then walks out the door, expecting me to follow. I do, catching up to him quickly.

He glances down, smirking.

I look up, fighting my blush.

We walk side by side in a comfortable silence as he leads me through the castle, toward some unknown destination. He is finally letting me in on one of his secrets.

Friends.

Is that what this is?

Is this what having a friend feels like?

I like it, I realize quickly. I like having someone by my side. I like feeling like I'm part of something, like I'm privy to someone's secrets, like they're privy to mine. For the briefest moment, I know what it would feel like to belong.

Cole doesn't stop until he's taken me up a winding staircase, through a heavy wooden door, and out to an overlook at the top of the castle. My breath catches almost immediately as I take in the scene.

We're at the end of the world.

Not really, but that's what it feels like when I look out toward a new view of the town I've never seen before. The window from my room looks in the opposite direction, toward the front entrance to the town and beyond into the mountains. But from here I see the back gardens of the castle. They're formally designed in intricate patterns, but time has turned them wild, as it seems to have done with everything else in this place. Yet the gardens aren't what has drawn my eye. I look behind them, gaze following the winding streets full of homes, all the way to the edge of the city wall. And beyond it, there is nothing but empty space.

The ground has fallen away.

I see sky and the distant hue of grassy fields far, far below.

There are no mountains.

There is nothing but what I imagine must be an impossibly steep cliff stretching down to new land hundreds of feet lower. And the truly strange part is that the cliff does not fall away in a straight line. No. The land disappears along the same curved edge of the crumbling city wall, wholly unnatural in its arch. And I know immediately this must have happened on the day of the earthquake.

Somehow, Cole's magic was able to protect his home, to keep the land within the city wall from disappearing. But the mountains that used to be beyond that back edge of the town vanished during the earthquake, merging with the flatlands of Earth in a bizarre seam.

My father and the base can't be too far off.

They must be out there on the edge of the horizon, just far enough away that when I used to gaze at these mountains as a little girl, I never noticed how strangely they rose from the ground.

"Ten years ago," Cole begins softly, drawing my attention from the vista, "I was still just a prince."

He leans casually with his forearms on the balcony, slightly hunched over. But his eyes are anything but casual. They're as hard as steel, flashing like metal glinting in the sun right before a deadly strike. He's not looking at the same view I am, he's seeing something else, something locked away in his memories, something terrible. And I want so badly to reach out and comfort him, to simply place my hand on his shoulder, to let him know he's not alone.

But I don't. Because his eyes are glazed over. He's in another world. And I don't want to pull him out of it before he's finished saying whatever it is he brought me here to say.

"My father was still alive," he continues, voice rumbling like soft thunder. "My father was still king. When the earthquake struck, we were at home. I remember the ground shaking so much that it knocked me off my feet. I remember changing forms midway through the fall. I remember even as a bear I couldn't keep my footing. But when it stopped, we were okay. We were fine. The city was safe, almost everyone I knew had survived. The ground outside the wall had fallen away. We thought it was some sort of strange magic. I wanted to explore, but my father had no interest in the outside world. As long as I was safe and his people were safe, he didn't care about anyone else. And then a few months later, everything changed."

He pauses, breathing deeply, finally blinking.

And then he turns to me, gaze questioning as it travels down the length of my body and back up, examining every inch of me with those piercing eyes, determining if I'm worthy of this confession.

I don't move.

I'm afraid that anything I do will make him stop.

But he just turns back toward the sky and swallows. "Some of the wolves came back after a hunt and said they saw a group of men with peculiar weapons camped out in the mountains. My father sent sentries to watch them, to keep an eye on the strangers. But all the reports came back the same. They were tracking something. They were creeping closer and closer to our home. They were searching for us. They wanted to hurt us. My father decided it would be better to act fast rather than wait for them to find us. So he took a group of our best fighters and pursued them. Five days later, four of the wolves who left with him returned, terrified and confused. They carried my father's body with them. It was riddled with small puncture wounds, holes in perfect circles that were too precise to be from any weapon in our arsenal. And I went crazy. I still don't fully remember changing into a bear and using the scent of my father's blood to find my way back to the men who murdered him. I don't remember slashing their necks with my claws in the dead of the night, I don't remember killing them. But I do remember gazing down at their weapons when the damage was done. I remember the moment I realized they couldn't be from my world, the moment I realized that the earthquake had changed everything."

He runs a hand through his onyx hair, sighing. Then he stands up straight, turning toward me as he pulls his shirt to the side. I notice the circular scar just below his right collarbone. I saw it the day before, but only now do I realize what it's from. A bullet. A gun. A weapon of Earth, not my old world. "I got this during the fight. I didn't even realize how hurt I was until I woke up in the snow, bleeding out and aching. The wolves saved me then too. And now it's a reminder of that day. It's a reminder of what those strangers are capable of."

My hand reaches out to touch his scar, but I stop just shy of making contact with his pale skin. "They're called guns," I whisper softly.

He releases his shirt and it falls back into place, covering the healed-over wound. "I know," he snarls. But I know the anger isn't directed toward me. It's just his gut reaction, his instinctual, animalistic response. "You've only ever seen me turn into the bear, but I can take other forms. One of them, if I concentrate very hard, is a hawk. And ever since I became king, I've been using that form to sneak to the town you came from and gather information about the people who killed my father. They've tried many times to make it through the mountains, but the path is dangerous if you don't know the way, and they're not the only ones with fine weapons anymore."

"You stole their guns?" I ask, surprised.

"I just evened the playing field."

Cole turns away from me, back toward the door leading inside the castle. He's done telling his story.

But questions burn the tip of my tongue. Everything he's revealed has just made me more curious about what he's not telling me. Like what happened to his mother. Like why everything within the city wall was safe from the earthquake. Like how he got his magic. Like where all the other humans went. Like who is that glowing woman locked away in that bedroom.

I push my lips together to keep them shut. He asked me to be patient, and I promised I would be. I can't betray the little bit of trust he has shown me, not right after he opened up for the first time.

So instead, I follow him downstairs, watching as he rolls his shoulders, releasing pent-up tension. As his muscles flex and coil beneath his clothes, I wonder what other animals rest beneath his skin.

"Cole?" I break the silence, ready to ask this one question that I might be allowed. What other forms can he take? What other animals?

But when he turns, his expression is so broken that I stop talking. All I do is reach out my hand, making an offer he can choose to refuse if he wants to.

But he doesn't.

He takes my hand and interlaces our fingers, gripping firm enough to hurt. But I stay quiet because I know he needs it, and I know I can take this little bit of pain if it means he can let go of some of his.

Eleven

After Cole drops me back to my room, I don't see him again until the next morning. He doesn't surprise me, doesn't scare me. Instead, I wake to the sound of a gentle, hesitant knock against my door. And for some reason, it brings a smile to my lips and a warm, fuzzy feeling to my heart.

"You can come in," I call.

He does, poking his head through the door first, gray eyes widening when he spots me sitting up in the center of the bed with the comforter wrapped snugly around me.

"You're still asleep?" he asks, puzzled.

I should probably feel mildly embarrassed. My curly auburn hair is most definitely in disarray. My eyes are still heavy with sleep. And when I turn my gaze to the window, I realize the sun is very high in the sky. But all I could think about all morning was how cozy and warm it was beneath the covers, and how I had nothing to do all day, and how for once I felt safe enough to just relax for a little while.

So instead, I shrug. "I'm awake now."

Cole stays in the doorway, filling the opening with his expansive frame. Something about him is more awkward than usual, as though all of his predatory grace has fled for the moment. He reaches up, rubbing the back of his neck, and I find myself holding back a giggle. "I, uh, brought you some food if you want it."

My pent-up laugh turns to a soft groan when I notice the small bag in his other hand. "More apples and dried meat?" After days and days of eating the same thing, my stomach yearns for new flavors.

But in the silence following my words, I watch Cole's entire person fall slowly—first his hand, which drifts back to his side, then his brows, which tighten into a knot, and then his nearly smiling lips, which drop into a frown.

"I'm sorry," I say quickly, sitting up, not sure what I did.

And then it hits me.

I'm an idiot.

All this time that apples and meats have been delivered to my door, I never thought about where they came from or who prepared them. I was too afraid of the animals dropping the packages outside my room to even think about anything else. But wolves can't tend to apple trees. And bears can't prepare meats to dry. And leopards can't bake any sort of bread. Only one person can.

Cole.

He's the only human I've seen.

He's been silently looking after me this entire time.

And how do I show my gratitude? By behaving like a brat and asking for something else. Maybe he doesn't have anything else. Maybe he doesn't know how to make anything else. Who would have taught him how to cook? The wolves?

"Cole?" I ask softly.

He nods, not looking at me, pretending to be tough just like I always pretend. But the tense line of his jaw gives him away.

"Has anyone ever made you breakfast?" I question.

His gaze flicks toward me then, alight with interest, and the clenched muscles in his neck release.

That's all the answer I need because we're friends. And friends don't act like spoiled jerks. Friends don't question someone else's form of kindness. Friends give back and show some compassion of their own. Friends see that spark of intrigue and get a twinge of excitement at being the one to put it there. At least, I think they do.

In a flash, I hop out of bed. I went to sleep in a soft cotton gown I found in the armoire, and I don't feel like wasting any time changing back into my T-shirt and jeans, which if I'm being honest, are starting to smell. So I wrap a cloak around my shoulders and grab Cole's hand, pleased when he latches his fingers tighter around mine instead of pulling away.

"Where's the kitchen?" I ask when we enter the hall.

Cole takes the lead, tugging me gently down long corridors until we reach a massive room that makes me gasp. Pots and pans line the back wall, all different shapes and sizes. There must be four ovens and ten stovetops. A huge table topped with a sturdy wooden block fills the center of the space and resting beneath the prep surface are every utensil and every bowl I could ever imagine needing. When I turn to look behind me, there are multiple cabinets filled with enough china to serve a hundred people.

My eyes find Cole's.

But his have grown hard and stormy again.

The questions die on my lips. Clearly, there was once a time when this castle hosted balls and banquets. When the rooms were filled and the halls were loud with boisterous conversation. Clearly, there was a time when people and not animals roamed the city streets. But what's clearer is that Cole does not want to talk about it. And I know in my gut it has something to do with magic.

But I made a promise not to speak of those things. So I open my mouth and ask, "Where do you grow the apples?"

His gaze softens. His shoulders relax. "This way," he says and nudges his head to a door I didn't notice before. He leads me out to an expansive greenhouse. The plants are wild and unruly, but I take a deep breath, letting their scents fill my nose, and immediately know there is so much here I can work with.

Cole watches me warily, as though he can sense the magic beginning to course through me. I keep it forcefully at bay.

"Do you have eggs?" I ask.

He nods.

"Could you go get some, please?"

I keep my voice steady as the magic builds beneath my skin, bubbling excitedly to the surface as the smell of so much vegetation continues to overwhelm me. Only after he's back inside and out of sight do I give into the temptation.

Immediately, I'm outside myself, traveling with the magic as it sinks into the dirt beneath my feet, kept soft and warm by the glass dome overhead. The apple trees Cole has been pillaging are where I go first, oozing new life into their tired branches. Rotten apples fall to the ground, replaced with brand-new glistening red ones. My senses extend further until soon I'm one with nearly every plant in this place. Lemon trees and orange trees blossom with new fruits. Potato spuds, radishes, and carrots sprout beneath the surface. Herbs pop to life one by one, basil, oregano, rosemary, and thyme. A garden of riches Cole didn't even know he had bursts to life beneath my magic. I bring new vivacity to vegetables that had grown weary and sad, and within all the magic, I hardly notice as I introduce new ones. Tomato vines ripen. Strawberry bushes rise in the corner. Raspberry bushes too.

I only stop because of the familiar pinch deep in my chest. The magic snaps back inside as a wave of fire courses through me, then a crash of frigid ice. Time strips away, stolen from my soul. And I stumble on uneasy feet, gritting my teeth to keep from crying out as I wait for the onslaught to end.

Another rose petal falls. Then another.

A few minutes later, I can breathe again. And with that painful reminder of the cost of my magic over, I push the power firmly back into hiding, trying to forget how glorious it felt to use it so freely.

When I return to the kitchen with a basket full of potatoes, tomatoes, herbs, and more vegetables, Cole is waiting for me. He doesn't mention the greenhouse. I don't either. We both pretend there is no awkward silence filling the space between us.

"What do you normally eat?" I wonder aloud.

Cole grins wickedly. His gray eyes flash, and I notice how his shaggy black hair falls over his forehead just a little when he turns to look at me. "Rabbits. Squirrels. The occasional bird or fish. Deer if I'm lucky."

Duh.

He doesn't know how to cook. There was hardly any food in the kitchen. And he lives in a town of wolves, bears, leopards, and who knows what else.

He's a hunter.

A carnivore.

The image of a bear ripping into the carcass of a deer suddenly fills my thoughts. I swallow, voice small when I ask, "So, you've never had an omelet before?"

His smile deepens, amused at my discomfort. "No," he answers slowly, shaking his head.

Under his gaze, I find myself associating with the rabbits, feeling caught, trapped by his unwavering attention. I clear my throat. "Well, it's no deer, but I make a pretty good veggie omelet. Hash browns are my specialty."

My mind wanders back to the base, to the small kitchen my father and I shared. Omelet day was a treat. There weren't many supplies to spare, especially for things like eggs and meats. But potatoes were plentiful, and I used to make them all the time, testing out recipes with the basic foods we were allotted each week. Once in a while though, we got eggs. My father showed me how to make them just the way my mom and I used to like, stuffed with vegetables, spicy, with flavor oozing from each bite.

"Can you show me?" Cole asks.

He snuck up next to me while my mind wandered, but now I can't ignore his presence. Heat from his skin funnels into mine, bringing warmth to my arm and a strange tickle to the back of my neck, a tingle that shivers down the entire length of my spine.

"Sure," I murmur breathily.

Air, I realize. I need air.

He's overwhelming.

I spin on my heels, surprising us both with my spastic movement, and start collecting items from around the kitchen. Mixing bowls. Knives. Forks. Anything and everything I think I'll need until my arms are completely full. Then I unload the pile on the table, using it like a barrier between my body and his, giving me enough space to think clearly.

I hand him a knife and half the vegetables.

"First, we have to do the menial labor," I joke, grabbing a potato.

For the next ten minutes, we work side by side in silence. But it's a nice sort of quiet, a peaceful one. Cole glances over every so often to make sure he is slicing everything the right way, but even if it's wrong, I don't correct him, not when he's concentrating so hard. I find my gaze constantly flicking over to observe the hard-set line of his pursed lips and the determined scrunch of his dark eyebrows. I glance away quickly each time, hoping he doesn't notice my stare.

When we're finished, I put all the ingredients in two separate bowls, one for the omelets and one for the hash browns. And then I reach for the eggs.

"Want to give it a try?" I ask, cracking one egg gently against the ceramic edge of a bowl and pulling it open until the yolk and whites fall easily into the dish.

"Do another one," he murmurs, focused on my hands.

I bite my top lip to keep my smile from spreading too wide, and oblige. Another egg falls seamlessly into the bowl.

"Okay." He reaches out eagerly. I can't fight the bubble of happiness rising in my chest as I watch him. But I've never seen anyone get so excited about making breakfast.

"Just tap it gently until it cracks and then pull it apart slowly so none of the shell falls in," I say as I hand one to him.

He nods.

Those smoky eyes land on mine for a moment when our fingers touch.

And then he looks down, rocking the egg in his hand for a moment as though testing out the technique. And then...

Crack.

In one quick movement, Cole slams the egg against the bowl in what he must have thought was a gentle motion. Immediately, it shatters in his hand, exploding over his ivory skin, landing half in the bowl and half on the counter, scattering shell remains everywhere.

I exhale noisily.

He flashes me an angry look.

Using all my willpower, I manage to swallow the laughter back down my throat.

"Try again," I squeak, forcing the words out and not one other sound.

Snarling, he grabs another egg. But I already know what's going to happen before it does.

Crack.

Shatter.

Explosion.

Same as before, only this time Cole slams his hand against the counter with frustration.

"Here," I jump in before he grabs another egg. My fingers reach for his, and before I fully realize what I'm doing, I'm pressed against his side, faces close enough to touch, wrapping my palm over his.

We both inhale sharply.

"Let me help," I say, amazed at how steady my voice sounds when the rest of me has decided to momentarily freak out. I'm even more amazed at how casually I push in front of him, so my back is pressed against his hard stomach. "Just put your hands over mine and observe."

My heart hammers in my chest as he bends over me, strong arms wrapping around my shoulders as his hands land on mine. His breath tickles my neck, stealing mine away. And then he leans closer, until almost every part of us is touching, and I remember again just how commanding his presence is, just how easily he can envelop me.

My fingers tremble. The egg cracks before I even manage to tap it against the edge of the bowl.

Immediately, I hear snickers. Little self-satisfied, arrogant, under-his-breath chuckles.

I spin around, furious, and do the first thing I think of—I smash the remainder of my egg right into his forehead.

Then I gasp as both of our eyes go wide.

Time stops.

Everything stops.

The only thing moving is the slimy yellow trickle making its way down the center of his previously pristine skin.

Before he has time to react, I run under his arm, escaping his hold and race to the other side of the table.

He growls.

For some reason, the sound excites me. I stop moving, pausing opposite him, and smirk as the egg yolk continues to inch down his cheek. We both keep our hands pressed against the butcher's block, staring at each other, waiting for the other to move. He creeps to the left. I move left. He steps slowly to the right. So do I.

But in the back of my head I know my time is running out. He's the definition of a predator, and I might as well be the definition of prey. It's only a matter of time before I'm caught. So before he can make his move, I reach for another egg and launch it at his face.

He catches it midair, reflexes incredibly quick.

But not quick enough. It crashes against his muscular palm and explodes, sending another splatter of slime into his face.

The growl turns to a roar.

I try to run.

Before I can even take a step, he leaps over the table in one unbelievably fluid motion, moving in a way only someone who is half animal could. Sturdy arms wrap around me, impossible to dislodge. I get out one shriek in protest before an egg cracks solidly against the top of my head.

It's my turn to growl.

I do. Not as menacing, maybe, and definitely not as natural, but I think I get my point across.

Apparently not.

A moment later, I find myself airborne, thrown over his shoulder in one easy effort.

"Cole!" I pound a fist against his back, but I think it hurts my fingers more than it hurts him. "Put me down!"

"You're supposed to be making me breakfast," he replies.

"I am," I reply sweetly. "This is how I make breakfast."

He snorts. "Well, this is how I make breakfast."

Then he's walking. And walking. The cool brush of wintry air hits my calves as he opens a door.

"Cole, where are you taking me?"

He doesn't answer. But the ground has turned to gravel that crunches ominously beneath his boots.

"Cole?"

No response.

I try to look around, but the blood is rushing to my head.

"Cole?"

And then I'm flying. I scream, but the sound is washed away as I land in a pool of ice-cold water that shocks my system to the very core. I gulp and gasp when I reach the surface, sputtering. I want to scream. I want to yell. My entire body aches for retribution.

Instead, I reach my hand up and smile as though the whole situation is one big entertaining joke. "Ha. Ha," I mutter. The words come unevenly out of my shivering lips. "Help me up. I'd like to eat before I freeze to death."

His eyes grow a tad concerned as he reaches for my hand, as though uncertain about his rash actions. I wonder if my skin is as blue and frozen as I feel. But I don't wonder for very long. When his strong fingers wrap sturdily around mine, I yank with everything I have.

Even a beast can be caught unaware.

Cole loses his balance, tumbling into the fountain right next to me. And when he comes surging to the surface, the first thing that greets him is a cold, wet splash.

I'm still shivering half an hour later as we both sit with our plates before a warm fire, wrapped in dry blankets. But even my chattering teeth don't stop the giggles that burst from my lips as I look up from my steaming eggs to find the dangerous, brooding beast disgustedly picking at the yellow goo still stuck in his eyebrows.

Twelve

The next day Cole greets me with breakfast in bed. Two omelets, nearly perfect. We eat side by side before the fireplace in my room, and I don't mention the few bits of eggshells that crunch between my teeth as I chew.

That night, I teach him how to roast a chicken, which he assures me tastes better than the way he normally eats it—raw.

The following day, he takes me to the library, a gigantic room that towers at least two stories high, and all I can see are books upon books upon books. He watches me wander through the shelves for half an hour before confessing he doesn't really know how to read. So we find a spot beneath a window, and I do my best to show him. At first he growls at his own incompetence. But it isn't long before I find myself curled against his side with his muscular arm wrapped around me as we lean over the page, deciphering the words together.

The day after, he tells me one of the wolves had pups, so we abandon the books. I watch from the corner of a cold cottage as he plays on all fours, barking and growling with the little fur balls. Every so often, his eyes find mine and he smiles just a little wider. And then I find myself pulled into the fun as sharp baby teeth tug on the edge of my dress, dragging me closer. Soon enough, I'm giggling as little pups pounce on my lap and scratchy tongues tickle my skin.

And from there on, the days begin to blend together.

Somehow, his hand begins to feel natural in mine.

Somehow, his touch becomes something familiar, something I crave.

Somehow, I begin to notice the subtle changes in his eyes. Glimmering silver. Stormy gray. Sharp steel. And those moments when the clouds clear just a little and the barest hint of midnight-blue sneaks in.

Somehow, I grow to understand the many vibrations of his voice. The harsh and aggressive snarl of his anger. The quick and light tone of his laughter. The long and drawn-out growl of his frustration. And my favorite, the soft and somber purr of happiness, so silent I almost don't notice the sound. But every so often, when we sit close by the fire, I hear that gentle rumble of satisfaction, and it warms me more than the flames ever could.

Cole shows me how to be wild and carefree.

I show him how to be civilized and proper.

Forgetting about my magic becomes second nature. Questions no longer wait at the tip of my tongue. I've let them drop away. When I find my attention wandering to that golden woman alone in that room, I imagine Cole's frown, I imagine how his eyes would grow stormy with hurt, and the thought disappears. When I want to ask about his mother, about why there are no other humans besides the two of us, I find myself daydreaming about how easily he makes me laugh, how I've smiled more in the past few weeks than I remember in the past ten years, how I finally have a sense like I belong, and the inquiries vanish. That's the price of his friendship. And it's one I'm willing to pay. For now.

So I wait until the dead of night, using the cover of darkness to cloak my magic, to hide it from him. The walls of my room have more flowers and more fruits than I can count. Under the light of the moon, I walk through the greenhouse, mind wandering absently as my fingers brush against silky leaves, and the magic seeps smoothly out. Recently, my thoughts drift solely to him.

He hasn't shifted in front of me again. I haven't asked.

Like my magic, that is his unwritten rule, the line he doesn't cross.

Sometimes, in those lonely hours, I yearn to push him across it. I wonder what will happen if we both fall over the edge. But by the time I wake to his smiling face at my door, the desire is gone. Joy bubbles up, filling my chest, pushing all the doubts away, and I'm reminded that things are fine the way they are, things are peaceful and happy and I don't want that to change.

Especially not tonight.

Anticipation swells beneath my skin.

Excited butterflies dance around my stomach.

And as I look in the mirror, there's a twinkle in my umber eyes that's never been there before.

I've been preparing for tonight for the past two days, ever since Cole told me about the winter solstice. He mentioned it casually—too casually. But his eyes were a deep, tumultuous storm that revealed far more than his words ever could. Something about tonight holds profound meaning for him, another secret I've yet to uncover. But he did tell me the castle hasn't seen a proper celebration in a very long time, and he thought his people deserved it.

So I came to my room and immediately opened the armoire, running my hands hesitantly over the beautiful gowns I had yet to touch. I tried them all on. Some fit. Some didn't, but nothing felt right. So I wandered the halls, opening doors and closets and drawers, until finally I saw the dress I have on now.

As I spin in the candlelight, I'm awed by how it glitters just as I imagined it would when I first laid eyes upon it. The bodice is black with lace that wraps across my torso, hugging it tight, and extending down my arms, leaving only my shoulders and my neck bare. The deep ebony gives way to soft silver as the skirt falls in waves to the floor. Diamond beads twinkle like a mix of sun and starlight as hints of gold flash, reflecting fiery flames. And the longer I stare at the glimmering chiffon, the more and more I see Cole's blissful eyes staring back at me.

I know exactly why I chose this dress.

I wonder if he'll see it too.

A knock sounds gently against my door, sending a flurry of nervous energy through me. I swallow, running my hands down the front of the gown, smoothing out wrinkles I know aren't there. Glancing one last time at the mirror, I stroke the ivory petals woven into my auburn hair, a little touch of spring in cold winter.

When I turn, the door is already open.

If I had any breath left, the sight of him would have stolen it away. Cole watches me with his hands braced behind his back. My eyes drift up along his ebony suit, fabric made of midnight, over the ivory skin of his neck, the soft peach of his lips, until they stop, trapped by those irises I see even in my dreams.

Hungry. That's the only word that comes when I look at him. That he's hungry for me.

The idea makes me shiver in the most delicious way.

"Do I clean up well?" I ask lightly, spinning around.

I don't even hear him move, but by the time I've completed the circle, he is right next to me, so close the edges of my skirt brush over his toes. Not a single thing about him is laughing.

"You..." he breathes, unable to find words.

Then Cole reaches slowly for my cheek, pausing just close enough for me to feel the heat of his palm, but not touching. My skin yearns for that soft caress. He flips his hand, so the backs of his fingers graze ever so tenderly against me.

The whisper of contact reminds me of a night that feels so long ago, when a stranger made me feel precious and wanted for the first time.

Before the memory has time to linger, he drops his hand, stepping away. For the first time in weeks, I can't read the emotion in his eyes. But he blinks and it's gone, leaving a wide smile in its place.

"Ready?" he asks, offering his arm.

I take it, swallowing any question I might have asked back down. "Ready."

He leads me to the dining room, which has been set for the first time since I've been here. Candelabras line the center of the table. Rose petals of all different shades lay scattered between them. Distantly I wonder why he chose that flower of all flowers. If it's maybe the same reason I chose this dress of all dresses. But the idea flees as I take in the meal placed carefully in gleaming silver bowls.

"What is it?" I murmur, awed. I don't recognize the food. It's not something I've taught him.

Cole is grinning, but there's an edge of sadness to his smile he can't hide. "My father's favorite. It's a stew we used to make together on the solstice. I haven't had it in a very long time."

But he doesn't say more. And I don't press him even though I want to.

"Where's everyone else?" I wonder instead as I take my first sip. Spices tingle against my tongue. The flavor creates a burning fire that as I swallow, sends a wave of heat to my toes. The perfect dish for a cold, wintry day.

Cole slurps a little as he brings the spoon to his lips. For some reason, that sound and the slightly embarrassed expression that crosses over his face melts me more than the stew.

"They're waiting for us," he answers vaguely.

I raise my eyebrows. "Waiting where?"

He shrugs nonchalantly, but his eyes shimmer. "It's a surprise."

He's teasing me.

"Why is it always a surprise?" I mutter.

He just grins.

I sigh, pursing my lips, and take another bite. "What are we celebrating, anyway?"

"The longest night of the year," he answers smoothly.

I stare at him. He glances at his food. I know he doesn't want me to ask, but the urge for just a little something more is too strong. "Cole..."

"The solstice," he begins, but pauses, searching for the words. And I know it has something to do with our promise, something to do with magic and the unspoken presence it always has in our conversations. I wish he would just tell me the whole truth. But he doesn't. "The solstice is the day my kingdom was first founded. Many years ago, on a long night just like this, predators who were once enemies decided to form one united people. And we've lived in peace together ever since."

What predators?

Why did they choose this night to join together?

How come?

But I know he won't answer. This is what he always does, offers just enough about himself to reply to the question without revealing anything at all.

Cole stands abruptly, pushing his chair back so quickly it nearly falls over. "Come with me," he urges.

His tone is pleading so I do, taking his hand, not saying anything as we leave the barely eaten food behind. It doesn't take long for me to recognize where we're going. I expected it all along.

Still, I gasp as we enter the ballroom. Cole starts down the steps, but I stop at the top, taking in the twinkling chandeliers and the newly cleaned glistening gold moldings all around the room. My eyes follow the trail of flickering lights around the sweeping space, meeting the hundreds of eyes reflecting those same flames as they watch me with their king. Wolves. Bears. Leopards. Birds. Foxes. A kingdom of predators who bow submissively before us in a swift wave. Cole looks over his shoulder, reaching out to where I'm stuck.

"Dance with me," he whispers.

My gaze drops to his. I don't understand the pain in his eyes. But I understand the hope. And it guides me to him. Our fingers wrap together, holding tight, and he leads me to the center of the floor.

"There's no music," I murmur shyly, conscious of the many eyes upon us.

Cole spins me toward him, grasping my small waist with his strong hand. The heat of his palm pushes through the fabric, burning as though there is nothing between us at all. His other hand still clutches me, holding our arms to the side. And then he leans in, close enough that all I see and sense is him, the broad expanse of his chest, the woodsy, wild smell that clings to him, the rumble of words deep in his chest.

He presses his lips gently against my ear and whispers, "There will be."

The first howl rises almost eerily in the silence. But another joins. Then another. The song reminds me of the one I heard deep in my soul the first time I stepped into this room, dancing with my memories before the sound of a distant laugh stopped me.

This time, no one is laughing.

Cole spins us, round and round, until the entire room becomes a blur of light and dark shadows, and he is the only thing I see clearly. His hands guide me confidently, pushing and pulling so I'm stepping and twirling wherever he wants me to go. His touch grounds me. And his eyes grow brighter and brighter the more we move. Every time he whirls me away, I search for those shimmering silver orbs, the center of my perfect storm.

The music shifts with our dance, tempo becoming faster and faster as howls turn to barks and yaps of joy. Cole pushes me away, catching both of my hands in his, and we spin. I grin first. Then he does. And before we know it, we're laughing, adding our own notes to the song. My head falls back as I close my eyes, breathing in the moment. Our hands begin to slip as the pressure mounts, but we keep stepping quicker and quicker, twirling more and more.

We snap apart.

I'm not even afraid as I stumble dizzily, off-balance in my gown. The world is still spinning. I can't make out up or down. But I know Cole will catch me even before his arms sweep me off my feet, still dancing as I reach up, holding the back of his neck. I press my cheek to his chest, listening to the rapid thud of his heart beating.

We slow.

He holds my waist firmly but releases my legs so they drift to the floor, leaving my whole body pressed against him.

I wait with my eyes closed until the room finally stops spinning.

When I open them, Cole and I are alone.

My fingers glide up into his thick, black hair. His eyes close as his body rumbles with that purr I like so much. With those stormy irises hidden, my gaze wanders, following my fingers as they trace the scars along his skin, the ones that have become so familiar I hardly notice them. I just barely brush the edge of the thick lines digging into his temples when his eyes pop open.

I should forget it. I should enjoy this perfect moment. I should push the question away. But I can't. It slips out before I can stop it.

"How'd you get these?"

Cole jerks his head away from my touch, stepping back as his hands fall away. Cool air brushes against me, bringing a shiver to my lonely limbs.

Whatever spell we cast, I broke it.

"We should finish dinner," he mumbles.

"Cole." I stretch my arm, but he moves out of reach. I turn away, hiding the hurt I can't help but feel at his rejection.

When I look up from the floor, my eyes land on an image that stops me.

My mother.

But I blink, knowing that can't be right. And I realize it's me. My reflection. I've never looked more like her than I do right now, in this gorgeous gown, with my hair pinned up, a grown woman. Tears spring, but when I look into my eyes, they're still those of a lonely child. I have her hair. Her nose. Her blushing skin. Her magic. But my watery umber irises reveal the truth. I don't have her wisdom. I don't have her strength. I don't have her courage.

I'm a girl playing dress up.

Always pretending.

Always hiding.

I might not be running any more, but I'm still too afraid to stand up for myself. I wanted happiness. I wanted acceptance. I wanted them so badly I didn't care about the cost, I didn't care how much of myself I had to shirk in the process.

Be brave.

A voice I haven't heard in ten years whispers to me.

My darling Omorose, you'll learn to be brave.

Her parting words to me. A promise I've yet to live up to.

I came to the beast for sanctuary. I came to find a place where I would be accepted for who I am. I came for answers. To learn about myself. To finally grow into the woman I'm supposed to be. To find my strength.

"Where'd you get those scars?" I ask again, softly.

And then I turn, standing upright with my shoulders pulled proudly back as I face him. I'm done swallowing my questions. I won't accept a friendship with parameters. I won't consent to half-truths. I won't tolerate a relationship based on lies any longer.

"Where'd you get those scars?" I say again, louder.

Cole takes a step back, stormy gray eyes begging me to stop.

But I can't. I won't.

"What does the solstice really celebrate?" I ask. "And why haven't you been able to celebrate it in years?"

Cole grits his teeth. The muscles in his cheek coil as his jaw clenches, sealing the answers away. But his silence just spurs me on. And all the questions I've locked away come surging out.

"Why won't you talk about magic? What happened to your mother? Who is that woman you wanted me to stay away from? Why are there no other people?"

One after another after another.

I lose track as they tumble through my lips.

By the time I'm done, my throat is scratchy from shouting, and I'm breathing heavy with exertion.

Cole's hands are curled into tight fists. His biceps bulge against the fabric of his jacket. His entire being trembles with pent-up rage. But I want him to let it out. To let whatever is holding him back go. To just speak to me. Anything but this silence.

His lips tremble.

They open.

Nothing comes out.

We face each other from two different sides of an impassable precipice. I want so badly to yank him over, but he's stubborn and stronger than me, and I know I can't force him to leap if he doesn't want to.

So instead I ask one more question. The most important one. The one that has somehow become more terrifying than all the rest.

"Do you trust me?"

It comes out as a whisper.

Cole steps back as though my words are a physical punch to his gut. He winces. And I can see the yearning to give in deep in his eyes. He wants to trust me. He wants so badly to trust me. But he doesn't.

I don't think he ever will.

And that realization stabs my heart like a knife. My head shakes back and forth, but I hold the rest in. I don't let him see me cry. I give him one more chance. "Do you trust me, Cole?"

Silence.

What is holding him back?

What secret from his past is tugging him away?

I'm not sure I'll ever know.

Before another moment passes, Cole's body ripples. The man disappears, replaced by the beast within. And he runs away. Leaving me in the middle of an empty ballroom, standing like a fool in a gorgeous gown, more alone than I've ever felt before.

Thirteen

I'm leaving for good this time.

As I watch the bear disappear behind the top edge of the steps, I tell myself that was the last straw.

It's time to admit my mistake.

I should never have come here.

I should go home to my father.

We should figure out a solution together.

So, I'm leaving.

But with my newfound strength, I decide there is no way I'm leaving without some answers. Which is why I find myself marching down a hall I know I'm prohibited from entering, toward a door I'm not allowed to open, to a woman I'm forbidden to touch.

When my eyes land on the golden glow still seeping from beneath the entry, a reckless smile spreads against my cheeks.

I feel wild with abandon.

And I like it.

Cole is nowhere to be found as I push my way inside and lay my eyes on the sleeping woman one last time. Her magic calls out to me just as it had before, tempting, magnetic as it pulls me closer. The longer I stand in the doorway, the more mesmerized I become. My brain turns to mush as my thoughts blend and fuzz, leaving bland awareness behind. The minutes tick by. I find that I'm leaning over her, not really sure how or when I moved from the door to the bed. My hand stretches for the shimmery film glowing just above her skin.

But I stop just before making contact. The magic whispers to me, urging me to touch her, to shift closer, to give in. Yet something deep in the back of my mind stops me, the memory of what happened last time, how my magic poured freely into her, how I lost control of myself.

"Who are you?" I whisper.

Cole's mother?

Sister?

I search for some familiarity in her face, but there's no resemblance. Her golden skin, her sun-kissed hair, everything is entirely opposite Cole's moonlight hues. And just as before, her features appear fluid, shifting every few seconds, pulsing from young to old, so one minute she looks sixteen and the next she looks thirty and the next fifty. Always beautiful, always refined, always glowing with an inner light. But also clouded by the magic.

"Why doesn't he want me to go near you?" I murmur. "How much do you know about magic? What could you teach me?"

Her power tugs at me, hinting that I can find all the answers if I just move a little closer.

Would she have answers for me?

Could she be the reason I was meant to come here all along?

I don't find out.

Something yanks on my skirt from behind, throwing me off-balance so I fall backward, landing hard against the ground. The pulling continues until I'm rolling across the floor, closer to the door.

"Cole!" I shout.

But when I turn, it's not him ushering me away. The snow leopard with the golden eyes tears at the bottom of the skirt with its sharp teeth.

"Stop," I order, tugging on the chiffon, trying to free myself. It rips noisily, but before I have time to stand, the leopard just takes another chunk within its jaw and keeps stepping backward, carrying me away.

"Let go," I try again. It pauses, watching me with those eyes that are too intelligent to be anything but human. "He doesn't want me here," I whisper sadly. "He doesn't want the real me, only part of me, and that's not enough anymore. I just came here to see if I could find any information about the magic one last time before I leave."

The leopard shakes its thick head, then steps forward, pressing its forehead into my palm until my fingers gently rub its downy fur.

"I'm sorry," I murmur, not really sure why I'm apologizing. Cole gave up on me. Not the other way around.

The leopard steps back gracefully, giving me room to stand. I take one last look over my shoulder toward the woman, but I realize there are no answers here, only more questions, and I don't have the patience to stick around and search in vain any longer. So I roll to my feet, despondently looking down at the shredded edges of my skirt. A small part of me thought about keeping it as a token of an evening that started out so beautifully. But I don't think I want to anymore. When I reach the end of the hall, I try to turn right, back in the direction of my room. I need to change. I need to plan. By dawn, I want to be gone.

But as I take a step, the leopard growls underneath its breath and leaps in front of me, blocking the hallway. I try to walk around the massive animal, but it's faster than me and easily cuts off any path I try to take.

"I don't want to see him," I say, because I know exactly where it's trying to take me. But it whines and bares its teeth in a frustrated sort of way. And then a new set of paws yank at me from behind, pulling on the skirt, and I turn to see the wolves. They grumble with the leopard, whining and growling as they pull me toward the left, toward Cole's bedroom.

I cross my arms in protest, but there's little else I can do as they use their jaws to forcefully pull me in a direction I really don't want to go.

I could use my magic.

But I don't want to hurt any of them. Not when I'm sure they're just following their misguided hearts.

And the closer they drag me toward their king, the more my underlying fury mounts, until I'm almost anticipating seeing him, just so I can yell and scream about what a beast he really is. The halls fade as I imagine the confrontation, pulled into the depths of my own thoughts as I formulate the perfect words to say.

I hate you.

You're a jerk.

What is your problem?

What else could I possibly do to make you trust me?

How could you just abandon me like that?

How could you leave?

Why can't you just accept me for who I am?

I'm not sure I'm even going to give him time to answer. I just want to make him listen to what I have to say for once. I just want him to sit and suffer beneath my wrath.

I'm so full of stifled aggression, I almost don't notice when we walk right past Cole's room. The door is closed, and I turn my head, looking back over my shoulder as they lead me away.

"Wait," I command.

They don't listen.

"Wait, where are we going?"

I know they couldn't possibly answer.

I know they are animals. I know I shouldn't expect anything.

But still, the silence just adds to my frustration. Another set of questions that go unanswered. Another time when what I want doesn't matter at all. Another incidence where I'm being pulled and yanked instead of politely asked and invited.

"Stop!"

I dig my heels into the ground and pull against their jaws, wincing as the sound of shredding fabric echoes across the hall. But they get the point. Finally, the wolves and the leopard pause, looking up at me almost apologetically, and they let go, taking a step back, giving me space.

I breathe for a moment.

Do I really want to do this? Do I really want to scream and yell at him? Do I really want that to be my goodbye?

Yes.

Yes, I do.

Rage back, I square my shoulders and turn around.

But at the exact moment that I take my first purposeful step toward Cole's room, a sound stops me. Stills me. Quiets the fury.

Whimpering.

At first, all I notice are panting screeches, gentle, high-pitched squeals. I turn back around.

The wolves and the leopard are watching me, and in their human eyes I see despair, but they aren't the ones making the noise.

It goes quiet. I look toward the end of the hall, searching with my ears. A soft, unnerving howl reaches me, mournful as it stretches on and on, lonely and somehow exploding with silent grief.

My soul is lured by the sound.

My feet move, pressed forward by my heart.

Another howl cries into the night.

I stand in an open doorway, just barely making out the silhouette of a single wolf weeping to the moon. He lies curled around himself, wrapped in the blankets of a warm bed, gaze focused out the window.

I've never seen him as a wolf, but I know it's Cole.

My anger vanishes the moment his broken eyes land on mine, and he howls once more into the night. I don't understand what he is saying, but I understand the shattered silver shards his irises have become, and I understand the utter loneliness in his call.

I step closer.

He watches me but doesn't move. Something in his expression is so defeated, so beaten down and overwhelmed, like he has nothing left to give, nothing left to fight.

I know he doesn't deserve my affection or my comfort, not after walking away from me tonight, not after leaving me alone. But I give it to him anyway, because I want to, because there's no one else who can, because my heart urges me to go to him even if my mind does not.

I crawl beside Cole on the bed, holding out my arms. He howls once more, but as he sets his head gently on my lap, the sound gives way to a whimper. And I realize he's crying. Drops of water stain my skirt as he curls closer, furry body wrapping warmly around me until we're both hugging each other. The downy gray of his coat melds with the silvery diamonds of my skirt until I'm not sure where I begin and he ends.

And we stay like that for a very long time.

Until his silent tears stop falling.

Until we drift peacefully to sleep.

And when I wake the next morning with the sturdy arms of a man wrapped around me, I know nothing will be the same. I know we crossed some line in the middle of the night. I know we've both changed.

I'm not at all surprised when I turn around still locked in his embrace and find those stormy eyes already watching me.

"I want to see your magic," Cole whispers, voice just as soft as the barely risen sun. "And after that, I'll tell you whatever you want to know."

Fourteen

I ask Cole to take me to the gardens.

We walk side by side, silent, wrapped up in our own thoughts. The sky is dark and gray when we step outside, mirroring the stormy look in Cole's eyes. The mood is bleak. But I'm not. I'm the only flower in a field of snow, opening up to welcome spring. Elated. Excited. Buoyant.

Cole wants to see my magic.

He wants to see the real me.

And I want to show him. Because he's only seen the harm my magic can do, that horrible day when I tried to escape, when I fought him, when I hurt him. It wasn't me. And it wasn't my magic. Not really.

When I glance toward him, I can't decipher his expression. He is rigid and unreadable. And I can't help but wonder what is going on inside of his head. Does he realize that this stony silence only makes me more curious? Does he even know that the brooding aura just makes me more aware of the many secrets he's trying to keep, makes me more and more eager to uncover them?

I've been honest with him. I answer every question he asks. I open up about my past. I appear to have nothing at all to hide. Doesn't he understand that it's far easier to keep a secret when no one thinks you have one?

I know he has no clue about the toll my magic takes, the curse wrapped up in the power. It's my greatest secret, buried so deep I sometimes even forget it's there. Sometimes I hide the truth even from myself.

Now is one of those times.

Because for once, I just want someone to see my magic the way I see it. Beautiful. Pure. Glorious. I once thought my father saw it that way, but I know the truth.

He loves me.

He knows my secret.

And for those two reasons, my father has no choice but to hate the magic, to loathe it for stripping hours, days, years off my life every time I use it.

But as I turn my gaze back toward the garden, opening my awareness, I imagine the look in Cole's eyes as he watches the power bring life to these frozen grounds, I imagine the awe and admiration I hope he'll feel.

As soon as I unleash the magic, I drift outside myself, traveling with it along the icy dirt, beneath the layers of snow, to the frozen roots struggling to make it through the winter. Cole no longer exists. I no longer exist. Magic is everything. The wondrous life it brings is everything. Roots extend beneath my touch, breaking through softening soil, stretching up into the sky. Colors pop as bright flowers shatter the gray mood of the day. The wild and mangled boxwoods bend and trim at my leisure until formal rows of evergreen diamonds and triangles meet in intricate patterns. And lastly, I grow the roses, winding the vines up the sides of the walled-in space until bright red shines vibrantly against the snow. Those petals are fresh and new and brimming with life.

But as I seal the magic away, recoiling and pulling the power back inside, leashing my own beast within, I can't help but notice how the rose in the center of my soul decays just a little bit more. I grit my teeth, holding my expression steady, hoping Cole won't notice the strain of my muscles as I fight the pain coursing through me. I don't look older, but as two more petals fall away, I know my time has grown shorter.

Twenty-five years, I remember my father saying. The most a woman in my family has lived after inheriting the magic is twenty-five years.

But when I open my eyes, inhaling deeply at the beauty laid out before me, the beauty I created, I know it's a price I'm willing to pay. I'd rather have a few more years with my magic than a lifetime without it.

Nervously, I glance sideways at Cole.

His gaze is on the garden.

I breathe a little easier knowing he didn't see the agony that coursed through me only moments ago. His eyes are wide, his mouth is slightly open, the edges of his lips twitch up. Perfect. Just like I imagined.

"Why can't all magic be like yours?" he asks softly.

I shrug, holding back my wide grin so he doesn't realize how happy those words have made me. "I guess I'm just lucky."

He nods, deep in thought.

I place my hand on his forearm. He flinches at my touch. "Cole," I murmur. "Your magic is beautiful too. I was afraid at first, but I'm not anymore."

"My magic?" He laughs darkly, under his breath. "Omorose, I don't have any magic, not like you do."

"But—"

He turns sharply, eyes bearing down on me and I pause.

"Omorose, I despise that magic," he growls. I step back, wounded. "I hate that magic with every fiber of my being. Your kind of magic is what destroyed my life. Your kind of magic is what has taken everything and everyone I ever loved away from me. That's why I couldn't trust you. That's why I pushed you away, why I wanted to scare you. What you just showed me is so beautiful, you are so beautiful, but if you knew the truth about your magic..." He trails off.

"What?" I snap.

He turns away, steps back toward the castle.

"If I knew the truth, what?" I repeat louder, stronger.

He stops, keeping his back to me. "If you knew the truth about your magic, I think you'd hate it too. And I'm not sure I can do that to you."

His words slice me deeper than he could ever know.

His rejection cuts.

"How'd you get those scars?" I ask grimly.

He turns slowly, gray eyes silently pleading with me.

"You promised," I say, voice low. "You promised you would answer my questions if I showed you my magic. And it's not my fault you didn't like what you saw. So answer me. How'd you get those scars on either side of your temple? They're deeper than the rest. And you touch them sometimes when you think I'm not paying attention, as though to remind yourself of something you think you might forget. And every time you pull your fingers away, the walls come back up, and you look at me differently, with something painful in your eyes. And I want to know why. I deserve to know why."

"You're going down a path you don't understand," Cole implores.

I remain silent. I harden my gaze for once.

"Please, Omorose." He sounds desperate. "If I tell you those things, there will be no going back. I'm not sure how you'll react."

I cross my arms.

He steps closer, putting his warm palms on my shoulders, gazing down at me with bright eyes that shimmer with a sort of inner light, and I notice the clouds have cleared to reveal the slightest hint of blue deep in his irises. "You are so different than any king or queen I ever imagined," he says slowly. The words fall over me like misty rain on a warm day. "You're so gentle and kind, so caring, so passionate. You breathe life into the world. You've filled this empty castle with your laughter. You've eased loneliness I never thought would fade. You've breathed life into me. And I couldn't bear to watch you fade away."

His words are so sweet, so pure.

But words aren't enough anymore.

I need answers.

"I need the truth."

His expression falls.

But then he looks at me and surrenders. "You want to know how I got these scars?" It's not really a question but I nod anyway. He lifts his hands, reaching into his ebony hair, brushing it back, and it's only then that I realize the three deep scratches on either side of his forehead are the same width apart as his own fingers.

"You?" I gasp, unable to finish the sentence.

"I was five when my mother died," he begins, voice hard with forcefully restrained emotion. "I barely had control over the switch. And when I found her body lying on the floor, contorted at angles I knew were impossible, I fell to my knees with rage and despair. And the claws came out before I could stop them, slicing me deep, marking me for the rest of my life, forcing me to always remember."

I peer at him. "To remember what?"

The look in his eyes takes my breath away. "To remember that beautiful strangers who seem too good to be true usually are."

I swallow, glancing at the floor. "I don't understand."

"Omorose?" he asks, voice laced with regret and resolve. "Do you know how your family first got its magic?"

My brows pull together. "It's my inheritance, passed down from generation to generation through an eldest heir, just like my royal title."

He shakes his head. "But do you know how they first got it?"

"We were born with it." I shrug.

He smiles grimly. "No, I was born with it. Your ancestors, they stole it."

My face scrunches in confusion. "What do you mean?"

He sighs. "I didn't expect you to know the truth. Thieves rarely recognize themselves for what they are, not in the harsh light of day. Only the victims remember. Only the victims keep the truth alive, passing it down from generation to generation so one day when the time is right, their children will remember and fight back."

"Cole, you're not making sense."

"I am," he challenges. "That's what scares you."

I don't realize I'm trembling until he looks pointedly at the goose bumps rising along my arms.

The cold.

It's just the cold.

So why do I feel nauseous?

Why do I suddenly feel sick?

In the back of my mind, something clicks into place. The magic has always felt like a foreign soul trapped inside of me, constantly fighting for release, only obeying when I'm pushing it back out into the world. That struggle has only strengthened with time. These past few weeks are the only ones where I haven't felt at war with myself, and they're also the only ones where I could use the magic freely, as often as I wanted, as often as it demanded.

But Cole's magic is something different. It belongs with him. Man and beast are two parts of one whole, interchangeable, perfectly in tune. I've witnessed his transformations. They are smooth, painless. The magic doesn't come with a price.

Cole runs his fingers down my arm, but even the heat perpetually brewing beneath his skin doesn't warm me. His cloudy eyes are concerned. I exhale, releasing the breath I'd been holding.

"They stole it?" I wonder aloud, fighting the spinning wheels in my head, allowing doubt and disbelief to color my admission.

But Cole won't let me hide behind ignorance any longer, and his next words stop my heart entirely.

"Haven't you ever wondered why your magic comes with a curse?"

Fifteen

I'm paralyzed by his comment. How does he know? How could he possibly know?

"You're shivering," Cole murmurs. But I can't move, not even to wrap my cloak tighter around my shoulders. "We should go inside."

He takes me by the waist, leading me back to the castle as though I'm a child who's barely learned to walk. I don't say anything. I don't have the strength to say anything. I'm mute as Cole brings me inside and gently deposits me in an oversized armchair. I'm silent as he ushers a fire to life and tucks a blanket around my shoulders. Then he sits opposite me. I'm quiet as I watch the flames dance over his pale skin, mesmerized by how they flicker warmly in irises that are usually so cool.

"Tell me everything," I finally whisper.

"I'll have to start at the very beginning," he murmurs, peering at me nervously, unsure of how I'll react.

I just nod. His eyes narrow with concern, but I don't want that right now. I don't want pity or comfort. All I want is the truth. The complete story.

And he gives it to me.

"Hundreds of years ago, in our world, humans didn't have magic. There were no kings and queens. The magic was concentrated in the earth and air, and in people like me, people made of magic. The world was populated with shapeshifters and faeries, centaurs and mermaids, even dragons. There were trees that spoke, forests made of magic, waters that could cure any disease, and spirits hidden within the ground, ready to grant small miracles. In that world, humans were nothing. They had no power, no strength. Legends say some were taken to be used as slaves, but most were left alone and ignored, considered unworthy of attention." He pauses.

"Until?" I prompt.

Cole glances at me, brows knotted together. "Until everything changed." He sighs, turning his attention to the fire, staring into its flames without blinking. "No one knows quite how it happened, not anymore. The best theory my father was able to uncover was that a human man somehow captured a faerie priestess and tortured her until she finally confessed a spell to trap the magic. He used the incantation and became the first human king, trapping magic within his blood and bonding it to his soul. The magic fused with his greatest desire, the wish to become undefeatable, giving him the most unbeatable weapon of all—the ability to control someone's mind. The priestess escaped, but no matter how hard she or any other magical creature tried, he could not be killed.

"Word of a human gaining magic spread, and people bowed down to him. He made them see him as a god, he coerced their loyalty, he controlled them. When his kingdom became so great that even his magic couldn't control everyone, he told his closest advisors about the spell and gave them great power as well. But once they had magic of their own, the king no longer had complete control over their minds. Without his knowing, some of the advisors plotted to overthrow him. They told their greatest warriors the secret of the king's power, and more humans stole the magic from the earth, trapping it and molding it to their souls, bringing their deepest desires to life.

"But the magic had to come from somewhere. And when the magic from the sea and sky was all taken, the humans began stealing it from the other creatures. The faerie priestesses watched in horror as the world they loved slowly fell to pieces. Faeries turned to flowers as their magic was stolen. Shapeshifters were trapped in their animal forms, no longer able to make the change. Unicorns were killed for the power in their horns. All the magical creatures left went into hiding, trying to escape the greed of the humans. And then the wars began. The humans with magic turned on each other. All the power had gone to their heads, and they were no longer content to follow anyone, not even the man who first gave them power. Battles broke out as they fought for territories, for their own kingdoms, to steal each other's magic and make themselves even stronger. Their children were born with the stolen magic in their blood, becoming powerful too. And only then did the first king realize his mistake, that power is a curse just as much as it is a blessing. So he returned to the priestess he once tortured and begged for her help to put an end to the madness.

"But it was too late by then. There was almost no magic left, too little for the priestesses to work with, nothing except for the magic fused to their souls, the magic they had been born with. And so, to save the world, they sacrificed themselves. The priestesses gave up their own magic, killing themselves so that with their dying breaths, they could put one last spell on all the humans who had stolen the magic. They were too weak to take the magic away or to kill them, so they did the best they could. The priestesses tied the magic to each human's blood in an unbreakable bond, sealing that union with a curse. Now, instead of limitless power, the magic was bound. Only one human could harness it at a time. New children weren't born with the power already flowing through them, and only one heir could inherit the magic. But whoever got the magic also got the burden of the curse, one could no longer exist without the other. And the curse gave the rest of us hope. If it was broken, the magic would be released back into the world, returning to where it was supposed to be. The first king spent the rest of his life traveling to the many kings and queens, using his mind control to steal the spell from their memory, until not a soul in the world remembered how to bind magic to a human soul. And then he killed himself, releasing his magic back into the world, confident that it would stay there.

"As time went on, some kings and queens died without an heir, and their magic was released back into the world. Some spent their lives figuring out how to break the curse, voluntarily giving up the magic in order to rid themselves of the burden. But many more decided the curse was a worthy sacrifice and kept the magic for themselves. The memory of those early days and early wars faded into myth. And eventually," Cole says, pausing to finally look at me before softly finishing his story. "Eventually, all human memory of how their royal families were created disappeared entirely."

I flinch at those last words.

My family was part of the third group.

I'm part of the third group.

We forgot.

We believed the magic was rightfully ours. And every woman in my family made the choice that the magic was worth dying for—we used it even as it killed us, and we passed it on knowing it would kill our daughters too.

"Do you know my curse?" I murmur, eyes on the floor.

"No," he responds slowly. "I just know you have one."

I open my lips to tell him, but only air comes out. How would he look at me if he knew I was killing myself in order to use my magic? If he knew my curse was that the magic stole a little part of my own life? Would those eyes ever clear of clouds again? Would they harden against me forever?

So instead, I latch on to something else he said. I hunt for more of his secrets so I don't have to confess my own. "You said they stole the magic from the creatures and the earth? That other shapeshifters were trapped in animal form? Is that...?" I trail off, glancing around.

We're alone at the moment, but Cole knows what I mean. Is that why all of his people are wolves and bears and leopards instead of people?

"No," he says after a drawn-out minute. He knows I don't want to talk about my curse, and for the moment, he's relenting. "What I just told you was only the beginning of my story."

"What happened?"

Cole cups his forehead in his hands, resting his elbows on his thighs. He runs his fingers through his thick black hair, scratching the back of his head while he takes a long, deep breath.

"I wasn't lying when I told you about the solstice," he says, words followed by the crackling of the fire and a permeating sort of silence. And when he looks up and meets my gaze, I think I'm finally seeing him for the first time. Cole is baring his soul. The storm is clearing. The beast is finally breaking down his walls and letting me in. "The shapeshifters once lived in segregated kingdoms, keeping to themselves, predators that never mixed unless they happened to be hunting the same prey. We numbered in the thousands. But when the magic started disappearing, everything changed. The humans ambushed our kingdoms, using the spell to steal our magic, leaving many of us trapped in our simpler form, no more than animals. The survivors went into hiding, trying to disguise the magic so humans wouldn't be able to take it away. And in the end, after the wars and after the priestesses laid down the curse, there were only a handful of our kind left behind. Most of the magical creatures of the world had been destroyed, and we decided that the only way to remain safe would be to create a kingdom of our own, in a remote place in the world where we would be left alone. My family has ruled that kingdom ever since the first solstice, until fourteen years ago, when a stranger visited and took it all away."

The golden woman.

My mind immediately drifts to her, to the magic glowing beneath her skin, the power that called to me, lulling me ever closer.

"She stole it?" I murmur.

Cole's expression breaks just a little before he regains control, hardening his eyes to steel. "We were celebrating the solstice as a kingdom, another year passed in secrecy and safety, another year of peace. Everyone was in the palace, drinking and dancing. Our joy as a people was palpable. I was only five, but I'll never forget when she walked into the room. Everything seemed to stop. No one had ever seen anyone quite so beautiful as this stranger with golden hair who almost floated as she passed us by. And then she paused before my parents, collapsing to the ground, landing in the form of a beautiful striped tiger. And only then did we all see her coat was stained with blood. Immediately, we jumped into action. Every so often, shifters would come from other parts of the world, looking for sanctuary. But no one had seen a tiger in hundreds of years. We thought she might be the last of her kind. We never doubted for a moment who or what she was. Magic is what keeps us in human form, our animal forms are our baser selves, and we all watched her shift before us. Why would we doubt? Why would we question? We had been safe for a thousand years, who would want to hurt us after so long?"

Cole's voice is cracking now. His fingers gently press against the scars on his temples, as though they give him strength and take it away at the same time. I slide from the chair, coming to his side in a heartbeat, pulling his hands away and filling them with mine. He holds tight, but his eyes are blank, unseeing. And I know he's not with me anymore. He's back to his five-year-old self, reliving every moment, the same way I do when I think about my mother or my sister, when I think of the way things once were.

"We didn't realize anything had changed until the morning," he whispers, tone utterly raw. "I woke up the same prince I'd always been. But my butler never came to my room to help me change. And the servants never brought my breakfast. So I went to search for my parents, and I found them in their room, sleeping late because no one had come to wake them. And instantly, we all sensed that something was terribly, terribly wrong. So we ran out of the castle, not even dressing, but it was too late. By the time we woke up, all the magic except for ours was gone. All of the people we were supposed to protect, all the shifters who trusted us, all of them were trapped in their animal forms, all of their magic had been stolen away in the night. My mother shifted before we could stop her, and as a wolf, she was faster than either of us. My father and I have always preferred the shape of the bear. By the time we reached the stranger's room to see her perfectly still, glowing form, my mother was already dying by her feet. I don't even know how it happened, not really. The only thing I know for certain is I was too late to save her, too late to save everyone, even my father, in the end."

"Cole..." I breathe his name, but there's nothing else to say.

His despair washes over me, tangible, and I recognize myself in that lonely desolation. We're the same, he and I. Different stories. Different lives. But somehow, the same. So completely alone. So unbearably lonely.

But as our hands grip tight and we cling to the warmth in each other's skin, I wonder if maybe, just maybe, this is the beginning of a new chapter, a new life not marred by so much grief, but alight with understanding.

Cole blinks and finds my eyes.

We stare at each other.

In the depths of his irises, the lonely years of his life flash by. The loss of his mother. The loss of his people. The loss of his father. The countless hours wandering these halls as the only one of his kind still left with any magic, the only man in a kingdom of beasts. I understand why he listened to my cry for help when he found me lying nearly dead in that field—he recognized himself in me. I understand why he tried to frighten me away—he recognized her in me, the glowing woman who stole the lives of nearly everyone he loved. My magic is everything he hates. I'm everything he hates. But I'm something else too.

Salvation.

I know because it's what I see when I look at him.

Someone I could finally belong to.

"I want to get rid of it."

The words come smoothly to my lips. Weeks ago I said them to my father, but I never truly meant them until right now, staring into his midnight eyes, clear and sparkling with stars.

I don't need the magic if I have him. He makes me want something better, something more.

He makes me want time—a lifetime of his fingers wrapped in mine, his gaze watching me, his warmth seeping into my skin, his touch whispering that I'm right where I'm supposed to be.

The seconds cease to exist when he tugs gently on my hands, bringing me smoothly onto his lap. Cole is my small pocket of infinity. Everything stops when he trails his fingers up the lace still covering my arms. I can't breathe as his caress brushes over the bare skin of my shoulders. The bloom in my soul expands as though I've found a new sun and I lean into him, hungry for more of this glow spreading through me. Cole's thumb finds the line of my cheekbone, tracing it as his other palm cups the back of my neck. We drift closer, pulled by an invisible force that's stronger than any other magic I've ever known.

When his lips touch mine, gentle and unsure, it feels like coming home for the first time in a decade.

I'm not afraid.

I'm not alone.

I'm empowered.

I'm brave.

My hands find his scars and brush over them softly, as though I can wipe the pain away, then I pull him closer.

I close the distance between us.

I force his doubts to vanish.

"Omorose," he growls against my lips, and it's a new purr I've never heard before. Desperate and passionate. Wild and untamed. Beastly.

Our movements become urgent.

Eager.

We explore, finding our true selves for the first time in each other.

Sixteen

Kissing Cole is my new magic. Just as addictive. Just as thrilling. Just as all-consuming.

Only this sort of magic holds no curse, no pain, no dark side. Instead, it makes everything light. And we spend the rest of the day discovering the source of this newfound power, letting our touches linger, our gazes deepen, our connection strengthen.

We sit in front of the fire long after the flames die out, creating our own source of heat, hardly noticing as the sky outside darkens. Only the rumbling of both our stomachs manages to distract us enough to move locations. But every nook in the hallway provides the perfect spot for a stolen moment.

Or two.

Or three.

Cooking dinner takes twice as long as usual. Cole slips behind me while I'm cutting vegetables, wrapping his arms around my waist and placing an innocent kiss at the base of my neck. I forget the food, spinning into that embrace. Before long, I'm sitting on the counter with my arms draped over him, distracted by the taste of him. And after my third straight failed attempt to finish chopping the carrots, I finally kick him out of the kitchen.

An hour later, I find him before the same fireplace. Only this time, the room is lit with a hundred glimmering candles, and a whole nest of pillows and blankets rest in the center of the circle where he's waiting for me with the book we've been reading together. Not surprisingly, the food gets cold before we manage to eat it.

We don't talk about the magic again. We talk about everything else. Cole tells me the few memories he has left of his mother, the pepper-gray color of her fur, the hearty tone of her laugh, the many hours she spent coaxing him out of the bear cub and into the wolf pup that looked like her. But it was no use, according to Cole. He's always been his father's son. Same quick temper. Same onyx hair. Same smoky eyes. And the years they spent together before the earthquake, years where they were the only two true shapeshifters left, only solidified that bond. His father taught him to hunt as a man and a beast. How to track. How to survive in the wilderness and how to rule a kingdom that had become wild. The wolves that still linger in the palace halls are his uncles and cousins, the only family he has left. The leopard with golden eyes was once his mother's closest friend, and like Cole, she still holds a lifetime of guilt for not being quick enough to save either of his parents. The older animals, he says, still remember who they were. It's the newborn pups who worry him the most, who he fears might never find the human counterparts hiding deep within their souls.

The hours fly by.

Kissing.

Touching.

Talking.

In no particular order, but a constant mix of all three.

The spell is only broken when my eyes drift shut in a sleepiness I can no longer hold off. With Cole's chest as my pillow and his voice as my lullaby, I can't help but drift away, completely safe and at peace in his arms.

Cole wakes me the next morning with a soft kiss to my temple. But when I open my heavy lids, rolling closer, I notice a lightning spark in his stormy eyes. I realize our night of ignoring the outside world is over. Our unspoken agreement to forget about magic for a little while has dissipated in the harsh light of day.

"Come with me," Cole urges, pulling me to my feet. "I have something to show you."

He keeps hold of my hand as we walk down the halls and enter the library. I'm not sure what could possibly be here that he hasn't shown me already—not until he leads me to the far left corner and presses gently on the edge of one of the ornate shelves. It springs free of the wall, opening up to a room I've never seen before, a hidden hole in the wall that is covered from floor to ceiling in loose papers, scrolls, and half-open books. There's a wooden desk in the center completely hidden beneath scribbled notes. There's a map hanging on the wall, highlighted and spotted with places I don't recognize. And as I step closer, there's one word written over and over again, shouting out at me.

Magic.

"Cole, what is this place?"

He walks in front of me, breathing deeply as his eyes, glistening mistily, roam over every inch of the room. "This is my father's study." He sighs, brushing his fingers over a coarse sheet of paper, running his hand across long-dried ink. "And I haven't been here in years."

"Why not?" I ask gently, seeing a spark of pain cross over his features.

Cole runs his hand through his hair, exhaling heavily. I step closer, wrapping my arm around his torso. He curls into my touch, hugging me in a tight embrace. He surrounds me, yet at the same time, I shield him from the ache. I'm so small that he tucks the top of my head into the nook below his chin, and when he speaks, his jaw presses gently into my hair.

"In those early days," he says hoarsely, "my father and I didn't know what to do. In the course of an evening, we went from a purely happy kingdom to a city of lost souls.

My mother was dead. All of our people were trapped in their animal forms, their magic stripped away. And I was just a child, barely five, not yet old enough to help ease my father's burdens. He spent the first few weeks doing his best to empty all the bottles of ale still left in city walls. Sometimes there were glimmers of his old self, but mostly I knew to stay away. And then, after a few months, something changed. He stopped drinking. He moved with new purpose, new vigor. And I didn't understand until he brought me here."

Cole releases me, stepping through the small study, picking through the papers and holding them out for me to see. "He thought he could find a way to bring them back. My father, like me, favored the form of the bear. But his mother was a hawk shifter, and she had taught him how to take that form as well. While I slept, he disappeared into the night, sometimes not returning for days. But every time he came back there was more life in his eyes, more of the man I remembered. He was searching the outside world for clues, sneaking into palaces, stealing any information he could find on the magic. He always meant to tell me more about it when I was older. He always meant to teach me to read the scrolls and write notes alongside him. But then the earthquake happened, and he, well…"

"He died," I whisper.

Cole shrugs, trying to be strong, but his lips pull thin. The muscles in his jaw clench.

"I used to come here. I used to try to decipher the clues he left behind. But, well, you know." He smirks, finding my eyes. "I'm not the most patient person, and it didn't take very long for just the thought of this room and the puzzles here to frustrate me enough to initiate a shift. Instead, I started focusing on things I could actually understand. I started spying on the people of Earth, learning about their weapons, using my own eyes to gather information. I replaced one enemy with another. I stopped trying to find ways to save my people, and instead busied myself with keeping them safe in this new world."

He pauses, lifting one brow in my direction.

I grin. "Until I showed up and ruined your plans?"

His lips twitch, but the storm in his eyes deepens, betraying the emotion behind his words. "But then I saw you that night. I was flying over the field, and I looked down, mesmerized as the grass turned greener, as flowers eased open, filling a black night with bright color, as the trees stretched higher. You were motionless on the ground when I landed close by. Even from a distance, I noticed the tears staining your cheeks. I smelled the salt on your skin. I tasted your pain on the breeze. And I wondered why such a beautiful person looked so alone and afraid. So I brought you back with me, I wanted to save you, to help you."

I put my hands on my hips, unable to stop myself from teasing him just a little. "So you decided the best way to help me would be to terrify me?"

Cole bares his teeth, growling lightly. "You're never going to let that go, are you?"

"No," I answer smoothly. He leaps across the room, picking me easily off the ground and swinging me in a wide circle, nibbling at my neck until I'm laughing.

"Okay, okay," I relent.

He puts me down but doesn't let go. Instead, he spins me in his arms and steps back, sitting against the table so we're at the same height. I nestle between his legs while his hands find my hips.

"I hate that you thought I was laughing at you that day," he murmurs. I look into his eyes, finding them downcast, and put my hand to his warm cheek. "I was on my way to find you, to bring you some food, when I heard footsteps in the ballroom. And there you were, eyes closed, swaying to invisible music, clutching an old blanket around you like a shield. I stepped back, not wanting to disturb you, unable to stop myself from noticing how your skin blushed pink, how the sunlight sparkled over you, how alive you looked. For a moment, you reminded me so much of her, standing in the center of the ballroom, so perfect. Too perfect. And it terrified me." He sighs, shoulders hunching in, gaze dropping to the floor. "I was laughing at myself, at how foolish I'd been to bring you back, how idiotic I'd been to think you might help me, how stupid I was for falling for the same trick a second time. So I did the only thing I could think of. I channeled my own fear and I turned it on you."

I step closer, nearly eliminating the space between us. "I want to help you, Cole."

"I know." He grips my hips tighter, digging his fingers into my skin in a way that thrills me. "You're nothing like her, Omorose. I see that now. Magic doesn't make you a bad person. What you do with it determines the sort of person you are. She used it to trick us, to steal from us, to exterminate us. But you, you use your magic to breathe life back into the world, to make it beautiful. To you, it was a birthright. You had no way of knowing your magic once belonged to someone else."

I shake my head. "That's not enough anymore." I look away this time. My eyes study the carpet, the floral patterns hidden beneath parchment. "My curse..."

I pause, taking a deep breath. Cole's hands travel up my back, easing out knots, bringing a shiver to my skin. But even with that comforting touch, I can't bring myself to fully admit the truth, can't admit I've been slowly killing myself. When I imagine saying the words out loud, they taste bitter and wrong. How did I become so addicted to the power that I was willing to die for it? How had so many women in my family justified that sacrifice to themselves? Their husbands? Their children? Their heirs?

"The magic, it's," I try again, but the right words won't come. And I realize, maybe they never will. So I try honesty. "The power is addicting. The more I use it, the easier it becomes to forget about the curse, to forget about the pain the magic brings. But being here with you, I've realized something. I don't need it. Not really. And I promised my father before I left that I would try to get rid of it and all the burdens it's caused for us both. I want to be free of the prison my magic has become."

He places his finger beneath my chin, lifting softly, pulling my gaze from the floor until I'm staring into his gray eyes, now streaked with blue. "The answers might be here, in this room. We can find them together."

Understanding dawns. "You want me to help you read your father's research? To find out what he learned before he died?"

Cole nods, self-conscious about his own limitations.

But I know the truth. After so many years of hiding who I really was, keeping to myself, cowering away, I know something so many people are too afraid to understand. Being vulnerable enough to admit your own faults, to open yourself up, to ask for help, that's true strength. And looking at Cole now, I wonder if he might just be the bravest person I've ever known.

"Where should we start?" I ask, excitement coloring my words.

He watches me warily, unsure about my sudden shift in attitude. But I'm already springing free from his touch, eager to begin. Cole doesn't even realize what a treasure trove this is. So much untapped knowledge. So much information about the magic. So much to learn about myself and the power residing beneath my skin. This is more than I ever dreamed to find when I decided to come here, and these riches have been under my nose the whole time.

My fingers jump from page to page, my eyes dance from word to word. Cole kneels down beside me, following my lead, grabbing the many papers from their messy spots on the ground and shuffling them into a single mound.

"Let's separate everything into piles," I say, not pausing in my work. "We can put all the scrolls in one corner, all the books in another. Let's make a pile of all the notes your father wrote and a pile of all the other loose papers. Maybe we designate a spot for everything we find relating to my magic and a different spot for anything we find about the golden woman and the spell she cast. I wish I had my highlighters. Or even a colored pencil, anything besides a quill. What I wouldn't give for a binder and some loose-leaf."

Cole covers his hand with mine, trying to grab my attention. But my mind is moving a mile a minute. How will we organize everything? What's the best way to take notes without all the school supplies I became used to back at the base?

"Omorose?"

"Mhmm," I murmur as the wheels spin. Maybe I use some berries to make a dye? Or I could just fold over the corners of important pages? Maybe use various pleats to categorize what we find?

"Omorose?" he asks again, tone suspiciously uneven.

I stop for a moment, finally looking at him, smiling when I notice the playful light in his eyes. He's not laughing, but almost. And then his brows pull together, serious.

"Do you really think we'll find anything?" he asks. And I can tell he's trying his best not to hope, to prepare for the worst.

I turn my hand over, squeezing his fingers. "No matter what, we have to try." He tightens his grip. "For my father, for your people, for ourselves. We have to try."

And for the next few hours, we do just that.

Seventeen

"I think I have an idea," I gasp days later.

We haven't learned very much, not yet, even after hours upon hours of relentless searching, of scanning page after page after page. There's almost too much information here. Wild theories about how the magic shifted all those years ago. Different legends about the mythical creatures that once roamed our lands. Endless accounts of interactions with kings and queens, detailing the different sorts of magic they possess and the curses that bind them. Fables. Stories. Myths. Memories. But nothing about the spell that can steal magic away, nothing about how to reverse it, and nothing about how to get rid of magic you no longer wish to possess.

Which is why I'm so shocked when I finally find something.

Cole's eyes snap up from the page he's been trying to read, finding mine immediately. "An idea?"

"Yeah," I chirp as my excitement bubbles to the surface, and I reread the page one more time, just to be sure. "Come here, listen to this."

He rushes across the room like a wolf on the prowl, moving with liquid grace, setting his arm across my shoulders a moment later. We lean over the page together. Normally when we're this close, I find it hard to focus. So does he. The tension is too obvious, the heat of a blush always gives my thoughts away, the storm in his eyes always reveals his too. That's why he was banished to the other side of the study, where the heat of his gaze is the only thing that can scorch me. When we're touching, research is the absolute last thing on our minds.

But not now.

Not when we might have our first breakthrough.

"This part right here." I'm giddy as I press my finger to the page, pointing to the passage I just read. "It's an old myth about a place called the Grove of the Undying. Legend says it was a small meadow in the center of a great forest filled with thousands of flowers that didn't fade or wilt, that survived floods and frost and even fire. Young lovers used to go there to pray for everlasting devotion. The ill would travel there to pray for long life. Until one day, it vanished. Gone in the blink of an eye. The forest grew in, leaving no trace of the beautiful haven behind. Almost as though it never existed. But it did, so what happened?"

Cole lifts one eyebrow, peering at me like I'm insane.

I throw the same look back at him. "What?"

"Nothing," he says too casually, shrugging.

I shake my head. "Don't you see?"

He breathes in deeply, eyes roving the room for any clue, any hint that might make him see what I'm talking about. And then his cheeks puff, and he exhales slowly, letting a long silence linger.

"Uh, no," he finally admits. I never thought it would be possible for a beast to look sheepish, but he proves me wrong.

"The flowers!" I say, waiting for realization to brighten his eyes, wondering if maybe I am crazy.

Cole just purses his lips.

My annoyance deepens. "Didn't you say that when the magic was stolen from the faeries, they turned into flowers? Just like how when the magic was taken from the shifters, they turned into their animal forms?"

"The flowers!" he gasps.

I smirk. Satisfied. "The flowers."

And then suddenly, we're on our feet, jumping up and down like little children, chanting the phrase *the flowers* over and over giddily.

"You really think they came back?" he asks, beaming.

I nod rapidly. "They had to. How else could a garden disappear overnight? How else could a thousand flowers vanish without a trace? One of the kings or queens must have died or broken the curse, somehow magic was released back into the world, and those faeries used it to come back to life."

"This means..." He trails off, overwhelmed.

I grip his hands, meeting his shining eyes. "This means there has to be a way to bring your people back. If the faeries got their magic back somehow, the shifters must be able to as well. It's proof that whatever that woman did isn't permanent. We can reverse it."

Cole sinks to the ground as his knees give out. I'm pulled down with him, landing hard on my butt, laughing all the while because my joy has to be released somehow. His pupils tick back and forth, processing words he never thought he would hear out loud, finally embracing the little hope he had kept hidden away all these years.

I want to let him have this moment.

To let him relish in this moment.

So I glance back down at the book, scanning the story once more. As my eyes rove across the pages, more words stick out.

Undying.

Petals no fire could burn.

Leaves no frost could wilt.

Roots no flood could drown.

Everlasting.

"Cole," I murmur.

He doesn't hear me. He's too excited, too lost in his thoughts, too far gone. My own thoughts whirl.

To the curved edge of the city wall—how the town was unnaturally kept protected from the earthquake when our magic world merged with Earth.

To the many reports I remember overhearing at the base—how the soldiers were mysteriously killed whenever they got too close to this kingdom.

To Cole's mother—how she died so quickly on that long ago morning, leaving him without any chance to try to save her.

Undying.

Everlasting.

"Cole!"

He blinks a few times, shaking his head, clearing it for me. "What?"

"The woman," I exclaim, on the brink of discovery.

But I have to know. I have to see her.

Cole is still watching me as I jump to my feet and race from the study, not uttering another word.

"Omorose!" he calls after.

I don't slow, but with his predatory speed, he catches up to me quickly. We don't say anything. I sense his curiosity, but there's something else, a shared awareness, a shared excitement. He knows that I'm on the verge of something amazing. And he knows exactly where I'm taking him.

When we open the door, blinded momentarily by the golden glow always seeping from her skin, I rush to stand over the woman. She looks the same. Motionless. Smiling just slightly. Sun-kissed skin despite the darkness of the room. Not a single hair out of place. Perfectly at peace.

I dive into my magic, reaching out with those sharper senses.

Immediately, her magic tugs on mine.

Immediately, my magic yearns to sink beneath her skin.

Immediately, my power aches to give her life.

I drift along the edge of where our two magics meet, holding mine back, exploring. And I realize that with my eyes closed, she feels no different than a plant. With my eyes closed, she is just another slice of nature yearning for my healing touch. With my eyes closed, she could be a flower.

There's only one explanation.

"Cole, she's a faerie."

His brows scrunch. "No."

"Yes," I cut him off.

"But why would she take our power? Faeries are born with magic, they don't need to steal it."

"I don't know," I whisper, knowing there is still a piece I'm missing. "But she's a faerie. Everything fits. It's just like those flowers in the Grove of the Undying. Nothing could destroy them. Haven't you ever wondered why the back end of your city didn't disappear in the earthquake? Why all the grounds within the wall were kept safe? Why the cliff edge curves in a perfect arch around your home, as though something was protecting it? I thought it was your magic when I first saw it, but you said it yourself, you don't have magic like I have magic. But she does. She stole all of the magic in this city. And she used some of that stolen power to keep you safe ten years ago, to keep herself safe."

Cole stops dead, face falling. "My mother."

My brows curl in with empathy. "That morning, your mother must have attacked her, and the magic lashed out. I wonder if this woman is even aware of what is going on around her or if the magic is just a protection spell guarding her."

"Guarding her from what?"

"Anything and anyone who would harm her."

"No, I mean why?" Cole snarls. His skin begins to tremble, and I know he's losing control of himself. But I'm not afraid of the fur and the claws. I grab his thick bicep, turning him toward me. Beneath my fingers, his clenched muscles relax and his thunderous expression clears. He takes a deep, uneven breath. "Why would she come here, steal our magic, and destroy our lives, all for a protection spell? Why would she trick us into thinking she was one of us? Why go to so much trouble?"

"That's what we have to find out," I tell him. "If we figure out why she was running, maybe we can figure out how to wake her back up, how to release the magic."

Cole runs his hand through his hair, scratching the back of his head. "I just." He pauses, dropping his arm and turning to stare at her. "I always thought she was a human queen. I always thought she stole our magic, and this was somehow her curse, this endless sleep. For fifteen years, nothing has changed. She just lies there, perfectly still like a painting, while our magic glimmers around her. I used to get so angry every time I walked by this room, every time I laid eyes on the glow seeping underneath her door. That's why I closed all the curtains, why I surrounded myself in darkness. Because even the sight of the sun became an unbearable reminder of everything she stole."

"We'll undo it," I say softly. "Whatever she did, we'll undo it."

He nods absently, silently raging at the faerie woman.

And deep down, a small part of me wonders if I deserve that hateful look too. Who did my magic once belong to? A misty forest? An innocent town of shifters? My power is nature, maybe it was stolen from a faerie? Is there someone, somewhere, who might also breathe hate at the mere thought of me? Who would lock himself in darkness just to keep from being reminded of me? Whose eyes would fill with the same amount of fury now pouring out of Cole's if they looked at me?

My skin grows itchy. Uncomfortable.

I scratch at my arms, but the sensation doesn't fade. It just grows stronger, until my fingernails are digging into my skin, scraping it raw. I hardly feel the pain. Not even as my eyes begin to blur. I think I draw blood.

"Omorose!"

Cole grips my hands, stopping me.

I begin to shake instead.

He draws me into his arms until I'm pressed flat against his broad chest, unable to see or sense anything but him. "Omorose," he purrs tenderly, placing a soft kiss against the top of my head. The rumble in his voice touches me everywhere. "What are you doing?"

"I don't know," I mumble.

But I do.

The itch wasn't skin deep. It was in my soul. It was the tingle of my magic, the prickling of power, and I was trying to claw it out of me.

This isn't about my father anymore.

It's not about Cole.

It's about me.

Now that I know the magic doesn't belong, I want it out.

I want it gone.

I'm tired of watching my time dwindle away to nothing. I'm tired of feeling the petals fall. I'm tired of sacrificing so much for something that was never supposed to be mine in the first place.

I step out of Cole's embrace, breathing deeply, unable to meet his eyes. Instead, I glance at my arm, still red and raw. There's one long gash from my nail, from that last deep scrape. I wonder if it will scar.

At the thought, my eyes travel to Cole's exposed forearm, to the ivory lines marring his firm skin. I always thought they were marks from a life of living among wolves and bears, but now I wonder if some of them are something else.

"Why don't we get some dinner?" he asks gently, as though I'm fragile enough to break.

I nod. "And then back to the study."

His eyes darken. "Why don't we take a break?"

"No." I shake my head. "We're not done yet."

"We can take one night off," he says lightly.

"No, we can't," I murmur.

A glimmer of worry passes over Cole's face.

But I don't give myself the time to wonder what it means.

I leave the room.

And I don't glance back to see if he follows.

Eighteen

"I can't sit in this room anymore," Cole says suddenly into the silence. "I'm going insane."

I hardly hear him, I'm too focused on rereading a scroll I've already read twice, searching for any hidden meaning I might have missed before.

Cole begins to pace.

A caged animal.

Every so often his feet walk through the edges of my vision. The floor beneath us quakes with his heavy footsteps. I ignore it, focus sharp as the edge of a blade. There has to be more in this room. There has to be something we missed. And I won't stop until I've found it.

I can't.

My back aches. My eyes burn. I'm not even sure how much time I've spent crouched over these old papers, scratching out notes, trying to solve this puzzle in my head. How can I get rid of my magic? Break the curse.

That's the only answer I find over and over again. Break the curse, and the magic will be released back into the world. But my curse is time. How do I break that?

It's impossible.

And the only other option I've found is death.

"Omorose," Cole whispers into my ear, breath tickling my skin.

I didn't even realize he had crouched down beside me.

"One second," I murmur, not pausing as I continue to scan the page for any desperate clue.

His fingers drift slowly from my wrist, all the way up my arm. Tantalizing.

I force the shiver away. Now isn't the time.

"Omorose," he repeats tenderly.

I don't acknowledge that I've heard him. I'm reviewing the tale of a king who died hundreds of years ago, one of the first to rerelease his magic into the world. Weather was his power. Storms raged with just the twitch of his fingers. But insanity was his curse. The winds he controlled were wild and untamed, just as his mind slowly became. Using his magic stripped a little part away, a memory, an emotion, an ounce of control. Something about it eerily reminds me of myself, of time slowly stripping, of the way my father desperately urged me to get rid of my magic, how he said my mother began to change, how little pieces of her began to fall away.

The king killed his entire castle in a fit of madness.

Murdering his children. His servants.

And when he came to, when he realized the toll of his curse, he put a knife in his own heart to finally end it.

For some reason, the story has stuck with me.

For some reason, I can't get it out of my mind. When I close my eyes, I see him. The mad king, covered in blood, clawing at his own skin when he realized what he'd done. The knife glinting in candlelight as it sank deep into his chest. The flicker of relief that must have passed over his eyes in those last few minutes of life, to know that he was finally free from the magic, the curse, and the trap it had all become.

Where did his magic go when he died?

Who had it belonged to?

"You're scaring me," Cole confesses, latching onto my shoulder, tugging me away from the paper in my hands.

I meet his cloudy eyes.

But all I can think is, how much time do I have left before my curse claims me?

How much time do I have left to find the answers I need?

How much time do I have left with Cole?

How much time do I have left, period?

Not enough.

"I have to keep working," I mumble.

"No," he interrupts. "You don't."

I try to shake out of his grip, but he's too strong. My heart begins to beat rapidly. I'm suffocating beneath his stare. "I need to, Cole. You don't understand. I need to do something."

"I know exactly what you need."

That stops me. I find his concerned stare. "What?"

"You need to let it out."

"Let what out?"

His thumb brushes across my cheek. "Whatever it is that's eating you up inside."

"How?" I sigh.

Cole grins. A wild streak burns across his smoky eyes. And then he takes my hand and pulls me quickly to my feet. "I have an idea."

I'm dragged from the study and across the library to a pair of doors leading out to the balcony. Cole pulls them wide open. A cold breeze stings my cheeks, forces me to take a deep, shocked breath. My lungs awaken at the touch of that frozen air. Every nerve in my body comes alert in a single moment.

"Yell," Cole says.

I glance at him. "What?"

His eyes twinkle like the stars just beginning to sparkle in the evening sky. "You heard me. Yell. Shout. Scream. Anything."

"No," I snort.

He deepens his gaze. "Do you trust me?"

A simple question, maybe, but for the two of us it holds profound meaning.

"Of course," I say without hesitating.

"Then do it."

I eye him warily as I follow him into the night, putting my hands right beside his on the railing. But I can't do it. I feel way too ridiculous.

"Cole," I murmur.

But he shakes his head and turns his face toward the rising moon, letting the silver glow brush over his skin. He glances at me one last time, before he lets everything holding him back go, throwing it out into the never-ending sky. When Cole screams, he roars, and the whole earth seems to tremble before him.

I laugh nervously when he's finished, knowing it's my turn.

But he turns to look at me, urging me. "Don't be embarrassed, not in front of me."

I inhale for a long time, trying to build up my courage.

Then I shout.

It's a pathetic little noise that trails off after an instant.

Cole raises his eyebrows pointedly. "Come on, Omorose. I know there's some she-wolf inside of you. I've seen her. You can't hide from me."

And he's right. Because that first little scream unleashed something in me. Something wild. Something that doesn't give a damn. Something that just wants to lose control for a moment.

Memories start to surge to the surface. Memories of all the times I bowed my head back at the base, pretending to be someone I wasn't. Memories of all the times the magic owned me, all the times it took over and took a piece of me away. All of the times I've ever felt trapped and afraid, alone and unsure, like a coward. All of my anger, all of my rage, all of my frustration, all of it bubbles to the surface until my skin begins to hum, coming alive.

I take a deep breath.

And I scream.

And scream.

And scream.

The sound wraps around me, going on and on.

I release everything.

I force it out, banishing all the doubts and all the negativity.

I throw it into the night and let it disappear.

And when I'm done, I'm heaving in air, but my heart feels open, my head feels lighter. I feel powerful. Almost dangerous.

"Nicely done," Cole remarks and I turn to find him grinning down at me.

But I don't want this feeling to end. I pause as an idea springs. Tentatively, I ask, "Do you think I could maybe break something?"

The corners of his lips twitch. "Sure."

His voice sounds undeniably intrigued. I follow him inside, and we pause by a glass display. Cole opens it, grabbing all twelve of the porcelain plates arranged inside, handing them to me in a stack.

I lift one. It's beautiful, painted with delicate flowers.

But that's the wrong image.

It only reminds me of my magic. And of my anger. And of the rage I've been suppressing that is suddenly undeniable.

I hurl the plate, watching with satisfaction as it crashes into the wall and shatters into a thousand pieces.

Then I throw another.

And another.

My arm is sore, but I don't care. It feels so good to just embrace the anger for a little while, to use it all up and let it drain away.

The plates are gone before I even realize it.

My hands feel unsatisfyingly empty.

"Is it wrong that I find all of this incredibly sexy?"

I turn to Cole.

The air around him simmers.

His eyes travel all the way up and down my body, slowly, taking in every curve. But when he finds my eyes, he pauses. "You're not done yet, are you?"

I want to give in to the temptations dancing in his sizzling silver eyes, but my fingers itch to keep causing some destruction. I don't really know what's gotten into me, but I kind of like it.

"Hit me," Cole orders.

"What?" I step back, shocked. "No."

He rolls his eyes. "You're not going to hurt me. And I'd rather take a bruise or two than destroy the entire castle."

"But," I protest.

He steps closer, squaring his shoulders. I always forget how much he towers over me, how truly intimidating he is—long limbs, broad chest, hard muscles.

"Just do it," he orders, totally amused.

I can tell he thinks my rage is adorable. I latch on to that annoyance.

Oh, I'll show him adorable.

I throw my fist into his chest.

Cole doesn't even flinch. Doesn't move. He's a wall of stone. The side of my hand stings.

I do it again. And again.

Blinded by the fear and frustration, I keep releasing all the pain. Has my life always been one big inescapable trap? I can't escape the magic. I can't break the curse. Will I ever just be free?

So I let go.

I lose myself.

I scream and shout and yell.

I let the wildness take over.

I embrace this brief sensation of freedom.

And when I finally return to myself, I realize Cole's arms are wrapped tightly around me, and he's whispering soothingly into my ear. My tears soak his shirt. I'm trembling. And when I hug him back, pulling him closer, he runs his fingers through my hair.

"It's okay," he whispers. "We'll be okay. We'll figure everything out."

I nod against his chest, sniffling, trying to regain control. But control isn't what I want.

So I lift my head, searching for a different sort of abandon. Our lips find each other immediately, colliding fast and fierce. I run my hands up the contours of Cole's chest, searching to close any distance between us.

The sound of a gun being fired stops me cold.

Cole and I freeze. The bullet ricochets off the wall before burying into a book, but the echo of that blast lingers, ringing through my ears, making the hairs on my arms stand straight up. A deadly sort of quiet permeates the air, stretching dangerously on.

I'm afraid to move.

The sound came from over Cole's shoulder, but he's too broad for me to peer around. So I glance up, only to realize his eyes are hard and edged with the promise of violence.

And then a girl's voice breaks the stillness.

"Let her go, or the next one goes straight through your skull."

Nineteen

Or the next one goes straight through your skull.

The words repeat in my head.

Twice.

Three times.

Four.

Each time, they sound more threatening. More dangerous. Cole's body trembles beneath my hands, and I know it is taking every ounce of control he has to hold back a shift. We're too close. He won't risk changing into the bear when his arms are still wrapped around me, when his claws could very easily dig into my skin.

But my magic hums.

Aches to be used.

And I'm still too high on the wildness that coursed through me, too eager for destruction, so I give into that pull. I let the recklessness wash over me, and I surrender to the power coursing through me.

The windows behind me shatter.

I push my way around Cole as the vines break through glass and soar across the room, roping around the stranger's gun and tossing it to the floor. I bind her arms and legs before propelling the ivy into the wall, knocking her head hard against stone. She blinks as though seeing stars, but I don't pause. I'm too consumed by the magic and by her words. Before she has time to fight back, the twisting vines are latched to the wall, growing steadily around her, securing her so she can barely move.

Everything is over in seconds.

I pant as I force the magic to shut off, gritting my teeth as the pain takes over. Fire and ice consume my heart. Cole catches me as I fall against him, watching me with concern and confusion. He still doesn't know exactly what my curse is, just that it hurts. But the way his fingers run soothingly up and down my arms makes the ache the tiniest bit easier to bear.

Another petal falls.

Another chunk of time slips away.

Seconds I could have spent with Cole.

Minutes I might have lost with my father.

Maybe even days, I have no idea.

All I know is that some of my life is gone, and this girl is to blame.

"Who are you?" I spit through my clenched jaw.

She doesn't say anything. She just stares at me.

I find myself mesmerized by the emerald color of her eyes. So brilliant, as though backed by fire. And right now they're full of an odd mix of hate and confusion that I can't even begin to understand. Her lips purse as the stare turns into a glare. Something about her reminds me of the sun, maybe the golden glow of her skin, made all the brighter by the dark, nearly black color of her hair. Or maybe it's her attitude, angry and blazing.

Steps echo from the hall. The loud pound of boots.

Everything about this hard girl softens at the sound.

And I realize why a moment later as a boy comes running into the room, crashing against the door frame, panting.

"Why." He wheezes. "Are you." He takes a deep breath. "So much." He exhales loudly. "Faster than me?"

The girl smirks arrogantly.

And then he looks up, searching for her.

It's my turn to gasp.

Something about him is so incredibly familiar. The icy blond hair. The fair, pale skin. The gentle smile that is rapidly turning to a frown as he looks around the room, eyes landing on the girl latched to the wall by my ivy. When his glance turns to me, my jaw drops. I would recognize those indigo eyes anywhere. I used to imagine them in my dreams.

I used to imagine him in my dreams.

"Asher?" The question falls from my lips, thick with disbelief.

His wide, light-hearted smile is back. "In the flesh."
He bows deeply, just like the prince I remember him to be.
And then he shrugs. "We're, uh, well, we're here to rescue
you...?"

"She doesn't need rescuing," Cole growls from behind
me, voice rumbling dangerously.

Asher jumps a little, laughing uneasily. "Yeah, well, it
seems I was a little misinformed. Now, if you would kindly
let Jade down, maybe we can all talk this out."

"Jade?" I ask. Isn't that a stone?

Asher just points to the girl on the wall who is glaring
at all of us. If it were possible for her to cross her arms, I
imagine that's what she'd be doing. And maybe tapping her
foot impatiently as well.

Two can play at that game. I step forward, cocking
my hip. "Will she promise not to shoot at us again?"

"Jade!" Asher rolls his eyes and throws a sidelong
glance at the girl, who is suddenly looking up at the ceiling
as though it's the most interesting thing she's ever seen. "I
thought we talked about this," he teases. "Speak first, shoot
second. Or, you know, shoot never." And then he turns to
me, still grinning easily, as though his face doesn't
understand any other sort of expression. "We're still
working on it, but she'll play nice, I promise."

"I can hear you, you know," Jade chirps, still latched
to the wall. Though I notice her muscles are strained as
though she's trying to break through the binds. Then she

sighs exasperatingly. "Besides, we both heard her crying and screaming. I thought he was hurting her."

Cole snarls quietly. "I would never hurt her."

"Well, you could have fooled me," Jade retorts.

They glare at each other. Stormy eyes meeting fiery ones, equal in strength and fight, neither going to back down anytime soon.

I look at Asher, unsure what to do. But he pleads with me silently, imploring with his plum-laced eyes. And I relent, using a smidge of magic to loosen the vines, remembering a time when those violet-hued eyes were the only thing giving me hope that someday I would eventually find a place where I belonged. At the time, I thought it would be by his side. But—

A thought bubbles to the surface.

"You died!" I exclaim suddenly, remembering the announcement back at the base, the one that made me realize I couldn't spend my life in hiding any longer. New York City had fallen, the magic holding it hostage had disappeared, Queen Deirdre and Asher had been defeated. So how is he standing before me now, very much alive?

I jump closer to him, pulled by a magnetic force. My fingers find his, latching onto his hands, yanking on him until I know I have his full attention.

"You got rid of your magic, didn't you?" I ask, begging for more information. "You released it? How? When? How?"

I'm too excited to think clearly. Too overwhelmed to realize how close I'm leaning into him. Too stunned to notice that two sets of furious, jealous eyes are now watching the spot where my hands clutch Asher's.

But he's not.

Gently, he shakes free of my hold, glancing quickly toward Jade with a hint of guilt clouding his expression.

I don't understand why until the thunderous voice behind me asks, "How, exactly, do you two know each other?"

My eyes find Cole's. My mouth goes dry. My tongue feels heavy. For some reason, I feel the sudden urge to apologize, to explain myself, even though I know I didn't really do anything wrong. But before I can answer, a different female voice chimes in.

"So I wasn't the last to know?" Jade comments lightly, too soft for a girl I already know is made up of hard edges.

"To know what?" Cole asks darkly.

Jade glances pointedly from me to Asher, then back to Cole, smiling sharply. "Omorose and Asher," she starts slowly. Her voice simmers, and I can't help but notice a protective edge to it, as though she's silently claiming her ground. "They're engaged."

Oh, for the love of—

"What?" Cole growls.

I jump in immediately, reaching for his trembling arms, getting close enough that I force him yet again to maintain control. His gray eyes are little more than churning storm clouds, dark and tumultuous as they look down at me. "We were," I say quickly, emphasizing the word were. "But that was a million years ago, in a different world, before the earthquake, before everything changed, before I met you."

His brows twitch, and instantly I know it's not fury he's feeling, but hurt. Deep, painful hurt. "Why didn't you tell me?"

I swallow. "Because I thought he was dead. I didn't think there was anything to tell. And even if he was alive, I didn't think it mattered. Not anymore. Not with everything that's happened, not with everything we've been through together."

"Ha!" I hear suddenly, and it's Asher's triumphant cry. "I told you!" he exclaims. Jade frowns. But at the same time, the corners of her lips are pulling up, as though she is secretly thrilled. "I told you she would say that. I told you she wouldn't care. I win. You lose. Next time we're home, you owe me one movie of my choosing. Something with a little less explosive destruction and a little more warm, gooey feelings. Ha!"

I blink a few times, utterly confused.

Jade doesn't respond, but her grin takes over. With her face soft and joyous, she looks so beautiful, radiant even. And so does Asher. The space between them fills with something palpable, electric, making me feel like the intruder.

Uncomfortable, I take a small step back, unaware how close I was standing to Cole until my shoulder presses into his hard chest. I lean into him, hesitant, hoping. Every part of me warms when he reaches down along my arm, searching for my hand. We clasp each other, holding tight. With his skin pressing against mine, I realize I was waiting for that small bit of contact, that unspoken signal that I've been forgiven. My heart feels lighter, and a different sort of heat passes through me as he begins to trace circles on my hip with his thumb.

Asher turns away from Jade, looking from Cole to me and back again. His brows pull together for a moment before he shakes his head slightly. "Why don't we both start from the beginning," he says gently. "You go first. Why does everyone at the base think someone called the beast kidnapped you? And why are you here looking very much at peace and not at all like someone being held against her will?"

"It's a long story," I mumble. But I can't help but notice how Cole has leaned away from me. His eyes burn the back of my neck.

"The beast?" he comments.

"Um," I murmur, biting my lip. "That's sort of what the people of Earth call you."

He snorts. "Really? No wonder you were afraid."

My tension releases and I smirk. "You did that all on your own."

He grins too. Our little inside joke.

"Okay, so he's the beast?" Asher asks, trying to make sense of everything.

"He's Cole," I jump in. "He didn't kidnap me. I just made it look like he did."

Jade and Asher shake their heads. Each raises an eyebrow at me, silently questioning for more. Even Cole watches on, intrigued by this story that I haven't told him. I take a deep breath. This is going to be a long night.

"You guys must be freezing," I say, ushering them toward the library door. "Why don't we all sit by the fire and figure out what the heck is going on."

They nod.

We walk as a group out of the room. Jade doesn't even try to hide it when she reaches down to grab her discarded gun, tucking it back into her pants. Asher tosses her a look but she just shrugs it off, staring back. They both remain stubborn for a moment, but Asher relents quickly, wrapping an arm around her waist and pulling her against his side. Jade is almost as tall as he is, and her long slim body is all muscle. He would never be able to move her anywhere she didn't want to go, so I know she leans against him willingly, because she wants to.

Without my magic, I would have been no match for her. She's a fighter. One look is all it takes to realize that. But it's just as obvious that Asher's not, he never has been. How did these two find each other? They're complete opposites, yet at the same time, deep affection ties them together. Love. Clear as a cloudless sky. Sparkling between them every time their eyes meet.

A little part of me wonders if they see it every time I look at Cole?

Every time he looks at me?

The idea lingers as we all take a seat near the fire. I settle into my normal spot, tucked into Cole's side. Pulling my feet into my chest, I bundle up, small and delicate compared to the muscular arm cradling me close. Jade and Asher don't say anything as they take their seats, but both of them watch me curiously. He stretches his feet close to the fire and she crosses her legs. In the space between their bodies, their hands come together, meeting seamlessly in the middle as though second nature.

"I guess I should start at the beginning," I say, breaking the silence. "I think we all remember the earthquake, and I know you both must have stories you could tell me of how that day changed your life, how it disrupted everything. But this is mine. On the day of the earthquake, I was with my father, traveling to see you, Asher."

Nodding, he says, "I remember." Then he pauses, frowns. "My mother was preparing for your arrival."

I want to ask why such a haunted expression just passed over his face, but I know I'll hear his story in time. Right now, they all want to hear mine. "When the ground settled, my father and I woke on one side of a dividing line. He and I were in an open field, and just fifteen feet away rested a town in ruin, a town full of things I didn't understand. Buildings. Clothing. Things like cars and phones. Things that were beyond my comprehension. We were terrified and alone, and the people of Earth captured us. For that first year, we lived behind bars, until my father offered to tell them everything he knew about magic and how to destroy it. They moved us to the Midwest Command Center, and in exchange for our information, they kept us fed and safe, they let us live among them."

I take a deep breath. Cole caresses my arm with his thumb, silently giving me his strength. "But something else happened on the day of the earthquake. My mother died, and I inherited her magic. So for ten years, while we lived among the people of Earth, I had to keep that power locked inside. I had to hide it, hide myself, pretend to be something I never could be. Normal."

Jade gasps quietly. I glance at her but she shakes her head. "Sorry," she murmurs, gentler than I realized she could be. "I held magic once, I felt it. I could never imagine keeping something like that contained. Never."

I scrunch my lips, aching to ask questions. What magic? How? Isn't she from Earth? Or was she a princess, like me?

I swallow them back down, continuing my tale. "But a few weeks ago, something inside me snapped. The general in charge of the command center made an announcement, he told us all how one of the queens had fallen, how the people of Earth had won a huge victory against the magic. I listened to hundreds of people cheer and chant, utterly jubilant to hear that someone with magic had been killed. And I just had to get away. I couldn't take it any longer. I wanted to embrace my magic, not hide it. I wanted to find someplace I could belong. I wanted to be free. So I ran away. But my father stayed behind, and in order to keep him safe, we tried to make it look like I was kidnapped, not that I left of my own free will. I didn't want anyone to grow suspicious, to think I had magic, to believe my father couldn't be trusted. I didn't know how long—"

I pause when I notice Asher's lips part. He doesn't speak, but I can practically hear the questions burning his tongue.

"What?" I ask. He meets my stare, eyes downcast with an unspoken apology. A fist clenches around my heart. Panic. "What, Asher?"

He winces slightly. "You said your father was there?"

"Yeah," I answer smoothly. "Actually, I'm surprised he didn't tell you I came here on my own, that I didn't need to be saved. Why didn't he stop you from coming after me?"

Asher turns to Jade.

She glances at him, biting her lip. An emotion I can't read passes over her face, lasting for a short moment before she looks away, cool expression returning. Cole's grip tightens, as though he knows. Asher spins back to me, gaze incredibly soft. The smile normally crossing his lips vanishes.

"What?" I whisper.

All the air has gone out of me in one fell swoop.

Because I know.

Without Asher having to say it, I know.

"Omorose, your father wasn't there."

My whole body deflates. The only thing holding me upright is Cole. Every ounce of strength seeps out of me, sinking into the floor, disappearing.

"They thought," Asher continues, unsure of what to say. "I mean, they told us he was kidnapped too. He disappeared a few days ago. They thought he was here with you."

"They thought..." I mumble, trailing off. The world is in slow motion, yet at the same time, everything is happening too fast. My mind whirls, but I can't speak. My movements are sluggish even though my brain zips at breakneck speed.

"Cole!" I screech, too loud, too high.

I'm on my feet. I'm pacing. Am I running? I can't process what's happening. The room blurs as my heartbeat turns rapid. I breathe quickly, sharp inhales and exhales. Alarm courses through me. Alarm and fear. I can't speak. Can't think.

I'm trapped by my own body.

Be brave.

That voice tries to whisper.

Be brave.

But I can't. Because it's my father. And he's gone. And my world would be nothing without him. He's the only family I have left. I love him too much to be brave. The idea of losing him is too overwhelming. Too much to handle.

"Omorose!" Cole calls fiercely. "Omorose!"

He's calling me back from the brink. I blink, clearing my eyes, trying to see through the panic overwhelming me. His hands cup my cheeks, and his smoky eyes gaze into mine with a fire that sparks me back to life.

"I'll find him," he whispers. "If he's anywhere on these mountains, I'll find him. Have faith in me. Trust me. Trust these words. I'll find him. And I'll bring him home for you."

I nod. But I can't find any words.

So I cling to his.

I wrap his promise around me like a warm blanket, comforting and secure.

Cole looks at me for another moment and then he turns, running toward the door. As soon as he's through it, he shifts, this time into a golden hawk I've never seen before. Wide, powerful wings, pump once, twice, and then he's out of sight.

Only when he's gone do I realize all of my hope flies with him.

Twenty

When I turn back to the fire, shivering from something much deeper than a chill, it's not Asher's arm that comes hesitatingly across my shoulders. It's Jade's.

I melt into her embrace, surprising us both, and collapse against her, knocking her off-balance. But her reflexes jump in, holding up my weight as she leads us closer to the fire. We sink slowly as she controls our movements, and I drift to a seated position.

The flames warm my frozen body, but my mind won't stop picturing my father's dead corpse buried somewhere beneath the snow on the mountains. Or his mangled body ripped to shreds by the wild animals not part of Cole's kingdom. The image switches between deathly cold, blue skin and red-hot, blood-stained snow.

Cole will find him.

I try to reassure myself.

Cole will save him.

But those two oscillating morbid pictures won't go away. And each time they flash before my eyes, they seem worse and worse, and more and more certain.

Asher comes to sit by my other side. He takes my hand gently, trying to warm my frigid fingers. And for a moment, his kindness makes me want to cry. Asher didn't need to travel all this way to rescue me, to risk so much for promises made when we were children. But he did. And genuine concern laces his eyes, genuine caring. In another life, he would have made a good husband. My seven-year-old self never needed to be afraid of a future with him. And in this new world, I know I'm still safe with him, even if the terms have changed. "Distract me," I whisper.

"What do you want to know?" he asks softly.

I shake my head. "I don't care, anything." And then I pause, biting my lip as I remember the cheers back at the base, the victory chants. There is something I desperately want to know, one topic that might actually pull me away from my dark thoughts. "How did you get rid of the magic?"

Asher and Jade share a quick glance and then both turn back to me. I'm not sure what just passed between them unspoken.

"What do you know about the magic? About the curse?" Asher asks.

I sigh. "Probably more than you. Cole told me everything. How a long time ago, we stole all the magic from the world and bottled it up inside ourselves. How the faerie priestesses used their dying breaths to lay curses down on all the humans with magic, to contain the power and to bind it to our blood, giving all the other species hope that one day the magic would be freed and released back into the world."

Asher frowns. "Huh?"

"Never mind," I say, shaking my head. "He can tell you the story later, it's not entirely mine to share. The only thing that matters right now is that we both know my magic was stolen, that it was cursed, and I want to let it go. So far, the only options I've found are breaking the curse and death. Since you're very much alive, I have to know—did you break your curse or did you find another way?"

I want so much for him to have the answer I need.

To say that he found another way.

To say that he uncovered a secret option number three, one I haven't in all my research been able to find.

To say that he knows how to save me.

"Do you know what my curse was?" Asher asks instead of answering.

My heart sinks. "No," I whisper, unable to fully find my voice because with that one question I know—he broke his curse. That's how he got rid of the magic, and that's all I need to hear. Because my curse is time and it's impossible to break.

Asher doesn't know how to help me.

I listen halfheartedly as he launches into a quick explanation.

"My family's curse was to never find love," he confesses, gaze focused on the fire. An edge of sadness latches onto his voice, a bit of darkness even this always happy man can't shake. "I'm not sure if you remember my mother's magic from when you visited our kingdom so many years ago, but emotion was her power. She could steal the feelings deep inside people's hearts, leaving them empty shells. She used her magic to take people's love and fear, their longing and hope, everything no one would willingly give her. By the time I was born, she was so wrapped up in the power, it had consumed her. She was beyond anyone's ability to love. And when the earthquake merged our world with Earth, I took the opportunity to run away, and I worked for ten years to try to bring her down. A few weeks ago, Jade and I did what I thought would be impossible. We put an end to my mother, and when the magic was passed on to the heir, we realized something—the curse was already broken. We loved each other, and the magic disappeared the instant we told each other that truth."

Jade watches him, smiling ever so slightly. But her green eyes hold a hint of sorrow. I know there is more to the story than they're letting on, and yet I can't bring myself to care. I know everything I need to know—they can't help me. And I'm starting to think that nothing will.

So I just nod, absorbing the words silently.

The quiet lingers, wrapping around us until the only sound is the crackling fire. My mind wanders to Cole and the mountain and my father. Worry creeps out of the hole I pushed it into. Worry and fear.

"I'm sorry," Jade confesses suddenly. I turn to her, eager for any diversion, but her eyes are on the ground. Something about her seems awkward in a way it hasn't before. "About before, with the, uh, gun." She takes a deep breath and meets my eyes. "I was under Queen Deirdre's thrall for a long time, and it's sort of hard to shut that side off sometimes, especially when I'm in fight mode. I really thought he was hurting you, I didn't know..." She trails off and then releases a soft, breathy laugh. "Anyway, I don't usually lose in a fight. That vine thing was pretty impressive. I never even had a chance."

"Wow," Asher comments ruefully, "apologizing and admitting defeat in the same breath. I never thought I'd see the day."

Jade punches him in the arm.

Lightly...sort of.

But Asher is still grinning as he rubs the newly sore spot on his bicep, and Jade just rolls her eyes, tossing him an exasperated look. I get the feeling that this teasing sort of banter is pretty normal for them.

Will Cole and I ever be free like that?

To just sit and tease without a worry in the world? No more magic, no more curses, no more mysteries to solve?

Nothing tugging at the back of our thoughts, shadowing every moment of light happiness?

"Omorose?" Asher asks, pulling me from my thoughts. But as I turn to face him, a sound in the distance captures my attention.

Howling.

My head whips around as my eyes land on the open door Cole disappeared through a while ago. I'm on my feet before Asher and Jade even realize what's happening. And I'm running, sprinting from the living room, racing through the halls, not stopping to see if they follow. I go faster and faster until I slam against the front door of the castle, unable to stop my momentum, but the slight pain helps pull me back to reality.

The doors swing open.

The echo of roars fills the town and I search, scanning the streets.

I sense him before I see him.

Cole.

But this time he is back in the form of the wolf, and he's not alone. His pack, the wolves I now know are his uncles and cousins, follow on either side. And across all of their backs rests a man I feared I would never see again.

"Papa!" I shout.

The body doesn't move. His limbs are limp and lifeless. My eyes widen in horror the closer the wolves approach. Each step brings my father's pallid color clearer and clearer into view. I've never seen his bronze skin look so pale and ashen. All I want is for those umber eyes that I inherited to open wide, to glance at me with reassurance, but they remain locked behind sealed lids.

Cole barks twice and slips ahead of the pack as another wolf glides in to take his spot beneath my father's body. A few steps later and he transforms midstride into the man who's come to mean so much to me. A few more steps and his palms grasp my shoulders, tugging me closer gently. Then he grins.

"He's alive."

I shut my eyes tight, fighting the sudden urge to cry or scream or do something in between. Pure relief shoots through me, bringing my entire system back to life. "He's alive?"

"Yes," Cole murmurs. The rumble in his chest comforts me. "He's alive. Barely. But I think I found him in time to save him."

And then the wolves are there.

They pause beside me, giving me the time to reach down and press my fingers against my father's impossibly cold cheek.

"Papa," I whisper.

He doesn't move. There's no response.

So I lean down and place a soft kiss to his wrinkled brow, unaware that I've begun crying until I see the sheen of teardrops glistening on his face.

"I love you," I whisper into his ear. "I'll save you."

And then I stand, stepping back. Cole takes my place, scooping my father into his arms as though he is a doll and not a full-grown man.

"I'll bring him to a guest room," he says, voice barely strained.

I nod, ready to follow. But then I glance over at the wolves. They're watching me like they already know what I'm about to say. "You remember what I need?"

They nod, more human than animal.

And then they're gone, off to fetch my water and bowl and herbs. Everything I once used to heal the wounds I put on Cole's body. Everything I hope will save my father now.

Asher and Jade watch from the far side of the entry, staring at the wolves with wide eyes and somewhat shocked expressions. But they silently fall in behind me as I follow Cole and my father down the long corridors of the castle. We end up in a guest room across from mine. Immediately, we settle my father on the soft mattress. I tuck the covers around his body, bundling him in the way he used to do with me when I was a child. I fluff the pillows before placing them beneath his head and feel his cheeks for any sign of warmth. But the only heat I feel comes from the fire Cole has just lit.

"More blankets," I murmur.

Cole doesn't need any other prompting.

He vanishes, only to return a moment later with a stack of wools that we together place over my father's still form. By the time I'm done tucking the edges, the wolves have returned, carrying everything I need.

There's not an ounce of hesitation in me as I call my magic to the surface. I don't care if my father wouldn't approve. I don't care if he would say it wasn't worth losing some of my life to save his. To me, there is nothing more worthy of my power. There is no other sacrifice I could be more willing to make. So I bring various herbs to life, letting the plants stretch and grow just so I can yank the leaves free.

Cole watches over me silently while I work, lending his strength as he presses his fingers into my back, massaging out the strain. His presence is more comforting than I think he knows. Those little touches keep me grounded, keep me focused. Without him by my side, the fear of losing my father would be crippling. Instead, I'm calm and clear. I'm brave.

My father jerks when I pour the first poultice forcibly down his throat. But I hold my hand over his mouth, wincing as his body thrashes beneath me. I don't release until he swallows. And then I pour the second. And the third. Each time, his reaction grows stronger. Cole has to hold him down while I work. But I don't stop. Even as he grunts in pain, I keep pushing forward. Because I know this is my only chance to save him.

An hour later, when it's done, my father has passed out from the exertion.

But his forehead is warmer.

The vibrant coffee-colored hue of his skin is returning.

His coal-black hair shines with a thin layer of sweat.

I collapse over him, utterly exhausted as I wrap my arms around his motionless body in a tight embrace. Beneath the covers, he still feels cold as ice.

"Please," I whisper.

A prayer. To anyone who will listen.

Cole runs his coarse fingers through my hair. "Omorose."

I turn, looking up at him, unable to move.

But he glances to the floor, and I hear their gentle mewling without having to look. It takes all of my energy, but I sit up and then fall against the back of my chair. Without pause, the wolves take my place, jumping up onto the bed and nestling against my father.

"They'll keep him warm," Cole says quietly. "They'll stand watch and let us know if anything changes."

I nod, but I can't look away.

My hand reaches out, holding on to the lump in the covers where I know my father's hand is. And even though I tell myself not to hope, I can't fight the disappointment that surges through me when his fingers don't tighten around my own. Shutting my eyes against the despair, I let go.

Cole's hand latches on to mine before I even realize I was absently searching for his fingers. I pull, and he steps close enough that I can lean my head against his side. Cocooned by his warmth, I finally let myself breathe for a few quiet moments. Everyone is silent. And I know they're waiting for me to speak.

"It's my fault," I confess.

"No," Cole urges, tightening his fingers around mine.

But I shake my head. "Yes," I protest. My voice is scratchy and raw. "I told him I would get rid of my magic and come back. I told him I wouldn't be gone for very long. He must have gotten worried. And I was here, with you, forgetting about him. While he was out there, dying to make sure I was safe."

My tone cracks in an ugly way.

"You can't think like that," Cole soothes. And I know he is speaking from experience, from years of blame and guilt over his own parents' deaths. But I don't believe him. Because I know the truth.

I was here, drunk on using my magic.

I was here, forgetting about the promises I made him.

I was here, falling in love for the first time in my life.

I was here, feeling like I might finally belong.

And he was there, alone in the cold, fighting with everything he had to be sure that I was safe and unharmed.

He was killing himself.

And I didn't know.

Didn't even think about it. Didn't care to check in on him and make sure he knew I was all right, that I was happy.

My father is dying.

And it is all my fault.

"Why?" I whisper, raspy. "Why did he try to cross over the mountains by himself? What was so urgent that he would risk so much to find me?"

"Um," Asher interrupts.

I spin. My eyes find his immediately. "What?"

Those indigo irises flash with revelation. "I know why your father was trying to find you." He purses his lips, glancing at Jade. Her face is cold. Those green eyes are as hard as her namesake as she meets his stare. But I know that lethal look isn't meant for him. It's caused by the information Asher's words have revealed, an understanding I lack.

"Why?" I plead, standing so quickly the chair tips backward. Only Cole's quick reflexes stop it from crashing to the floor. "Tell me."

They both look from Cole to me to Cole and back.

Finally, Asher sighs. "The Midwest Command Center, the general there, he's planning an attack. The wheels were already in motion by the time we arrived. Your father, he must have heard about it, he must have been coming to warn you, to get you to leave before you were killed."

Cold dread trickles through me.

Even Cole's hand feels cold.

"They've tried to attack before," he growls, voice low and fueled with danger. "They've never once made it through the mountains. In the ten years since the earthquake, no one has ever breeched our city's wall until you did tonight."

Asher glances at him apologetically. "They're not coming through the mountains." Cole frowns, waiting. Both of us hang on the edge of Asher's next words. But he doesn't elaborate. Instead, he and Jade share another quick glance, another unspoken conversation.

"Asher," I say slowly, voice just on the edge of wild fury. "If you care for me at all, if you want to honor the promises we were once supposed to make to each other, you'll tell me what they're planning. Now."

His brows tighten. "The magic," he admits. "Even if you don't think it is, it's evil. All of it. And it has to be stopped."

When I glance up at Cole's face, it's gone white, so pale that his scars have faded into his skin. All the blood is rushing from his cheeks. I squeeze his fingers, trying to let him know I'm here, that I won't let anything happen to his family, to his people.

"The magic in this kingdom, it's not what you think it is," I urge. "Even Cole and I don't fully understand it. We don't know what will happen if the person wielding it is killed, what will happen to you if you try to kill her. We're trying to stop her, but we need time to find answers."

Time.

The one thing that has never been on my side. And when Asher's soft gaze lands on mine, I know that yet again, time will be my enemy.

"They're attacking in two weeks, whether Jade and I make it back to the base or not."

Twenty-One

Their plan is so simple I'm amazed we didn't see it coming.

The general has never been able to bring troops over the mountains. Cole confessed he's killed many of them himself. Others were stopped by avalanches, blizzards, and storms. And the rest, we both think, were killed by the magic we still don't understand, the spell protecting that woman while she slumbers peacefully in bed.

But this time, they're not coming through the mountains.

They're bringing the mountains down.

One mountain to be exact.

One steep cliff.

The one Cole's kingdom rests upon.

For the past few weeks, the general has been sending soldiers beyond the front line, into the magic realm where the radar system is useless, and the electricity doesn't work. They've been scoping out the bottom edge of the cliff, searching for cracks, weaknesses, and fissures, mapping out the terrain. When Asher and Jade left, the general had already begun setting up explosives strategically along those fault lines—dynamite, bombs, old-fashioned triggers, more devices than I could begin to understand. But I don't need to understand because I know enough.

In two weeks, they're going to blow the mountain up.

And those of us living at the top are going to come tumbling down.

Simple science.

And the protection spell guarding that faerie might be able to save her from the fall, but I doubt it will save all of us. I'm not willing to take that chance.

We have to leave.

There's no other option.

Yet as I sit next to my father's bed, the very idea terrifies me. Because he still hasn't opened his eyes. Skin that was once cold has grown impossibly hot with fever. His bronze color has gained a horrid chartreuse sheen. In his sleep, he murmurs unintelligibly. And the only thing that seems to soothe him even a little bit is the sound of my voice.

How can I move him?

How can I bring him back out into the cold?

Death if he stays. Death if he leaves.

What am I supposed to do?

"Hey," a voice murmurs.

I turn to find Asher watching me from the doorway, but I don't say anything. I just return to my father, brushing the sweat from his face with a cold towel.

He walks into the room and takes the seat next to me. "How's he doing?"

I frown and shake my head. But I don't speak. The words are too hard to say. I can't push them through my clogged throat. I can hardly even think them.

"Jade is still with Cole," he comments conversationally, filling the silence. "They're figuring out the best escape route through the mountains, comparing maps and information. She's better at that sort of thing than I am, so I figured I'd let the two of them work it out." He shrugs, not at all afraid to admit his own weaknesses. "I'm better at reading people."

The way he says it makes me look up.

Those indigo eyes bore into mine as though he can see all the way to my soul. As though I'm exposed and there's nowhere I can hide.

And I guess that's what I've been doing in here.

Hiding from the decision I'll soon have to make.

"What are you hinting at?" I comment, getting right to the point. I'm in no mood for games.

But he glances away, eyes going to the pots filling every corner of the room, the many herbs I brought to life to try to help my father. "Do you think he would want you to be doing this?"

"That's not his choice to make," I reply smoothly, turning back to my father, but Asher traps me with his stare, examining my expression so openly that I feel the need to run. My heart pounds under the scrutiny.

"I thought that way once," he says softly, still holding me captive. "I thought that sacrificing myself for a good cause was my right. But it isn't. Not always. Not when other people are involved. You have to take their wishes into account. Their choices. Sometimes, the sacrifice isn't worth it. Sometimes, all it does is leave the people you're willing to die for with unmanageable guilt. Sometimes, it's a burden and not a blessing."

I shake my head. "So I should let him die? Why? Why should I have to live the rest of my life with the guilt of knowing I didn't do everything I could to save him?"

"Because he's your father."

I close my eyes tight, hiding from the words.

But Asher doesn't relent. "Because you know this isn't what he would want."

"What do you know about it?" I snap.

"Enough," he replies calmly. "Maybe it would be different if it was Cole on that bed. Or your father looking over you. But any good parent would put his child's life over his. Any loving parent would never choose to save himself if it meant hurting his child. And I know your father loved you. That's the only reason he would have risked so much to try to save you."

I lick my lips, swallowing slowly as I realize something.

Why does Asher think I'm sacrificing anything?

Why is he speaking like he knows my secrets?

Like he knows the cost of my magic?

My fingers turn cold.

My whole body freezes.

"What aren't you saying, Asher?"

He looks down and fiddles with his fingers as an unsure expression passes over his face, like he knows he's about to cross a line that he maybe shouldn't.

"I heard something a long time ago," he says slowly. One of his legs begins to bounce with pent-up energy. "I didn't remember it until you asked me how I broke my curse. Something about hearing your voice or seeing your face, it brought back a memory. You were five, same as me. It was the second summer we had spent together, though together is probably too generous a term. I was always chasing after you, and you were always running away. You were afraid of me, and I couldn't for the life of me understand why. So I followed you one day, and I overheard you talking to your mother about her magic, about the magic you would inherit, about the magic I was supposed to inherit. And I understood."

His voice is full of so much sorrow, so much pain. I reach out, placing my hand on his forearm. "I wasn't afraid of you."

He shakes his head, finally looking up at me. "It's okay. I don't blame you." He laughs softly, under his breath, in a sad sort of way. "I would have been afraid of me too. Who wouldn't be afraid of the prince who couldn't feel love, who would one day inherit magic that would steal everyone's emotions away, who would become king of such an unhappy place? I almost left after I heard you say those things. I told myself I would leave you alone, that I wouldn't bother you anymore. But right as I was turning away, your mother pushed your hair back from your face."

I suck in a breath. Suddenly I remember. "She told me not to judge you for magic that isn't even yours yet. She told me to give you a chance." My gut clenches. "She said maybe if you knew the toll of the magic I would one day inherit, you wouldn't want to spend time with me either."

"I know your curse," Asher confesses.

I thought those words would terrify me, but for some strange reason they don't. It's almost a relief to hear that someone else knows my secret. That someone else knows the full truth of who I am and what my magic is, yet still came here to comfort me, to talk to me, to help me.

Unfortunately, words aren't enough to save me now.

"Then you know it can never be broken," I murmur. "So in the time I have left, I might as well use my magic to keep the people I love alive."

"There was a time I thought my curse could never be broken. But it was."

I snort. It's a nasty sort of sound, bitter and harsh, but I can't help it. "Well, not all of us are lucky enough to have a curse like yours, Asher. Some curses need more than a kiss and a happily ever after. Some curses are made to stick."

He flinches.

But now that I've started I can't stop. "If you have any ideas, I'd love to hear them." My voice is acid, sarcastic and cruel. "How can I break the curse of time? How can I make myself live longer when the magic is slowly killing me? Have you found some cure for death that I don't know about? Some spell for immortality? Anything?"

I take a breath.

He remains silent.

The smile normally spreading across his face is nowhere to be seen.

"That's what I thought, Asher." The fight is starting to ebb. The sting of my own truths are painful even to me. "No one can help me. Not you. Not Jade. Not my father. Not even Cole. Love isn't enough to save me. I'm on my own. Just me and my curse, alone the way I've always been. So don't tell me how to use my magic in the little bit of time I have left. I don't need a lecture."

"You're right," he says gently.

That kind, caring sound steals what little fight I had left. My shoulders slump, dragged down by the hopelessness coursing through me. "I'm right?"

He takes my hand. "I know you haven't told Cole about your curse. If you had, he would be doing everything he could to make sure you stopped using your magic. At least, that's what I would do if you were Jade, or if I were Cole. But we're not. We may be engaged." He winks at me, and it's enough to make me smile. "But we're not in love. And I thought maybe that's what you needed. Just a friend. Someone to talk to. Someone who isn't quite so invested, who can listen to what you have to say without taking it too personally."

I let his words sink in, not sure if I should be offended or pleased. "So you're saying you came all the way here just to tell me that you don't love me and you aren't that invested in whether I live or die?"

He nods, open and honest. "Exactly."

I stare at him.

How can he say that with a straight face?

Is he joking?

Is he—

But then I notice his lips twitch.

Suddenly, I understand why Jade always has the urge to punch him.

"Asher!" I shake his hand away, annoyed.

"Okay, okay," he jumps in before I can say anything else and grins. "Maybe that's not entirely true. But I wanted you to be honest with yourself, to be honest with me, and I wanted you to know that I'm here for you if you need me.

You don't need to keep so much to yourself. You can talk to me about the magic, about the curse, and I won't say anything to anyone, not even Jade."

Part of me wants to thank him, but another part doesn't want to let him off the hook quite so easily. The latter wins out. "So, basically, you came here with the sole purpose of making me angry enough to tell you the truth, all the while knowing you have no idea how to actually solve any of my problems."

He frowns for a moment. "Maybe." And then his face brightens, pale skin suddenly as luminescent as the moon. "But," he retorts triumphantly. "There was a time in my life when I was exactly where you are now. I thought my curse could never be broken. I thought sacrificing myself was the only solution. And if Jade had never come along, I'd be dead right now. Not alive and in love and living my happily ever after, as you called it. So, the moral of the story is don't give up. Not yet. Because there's an answer somewhere, we just need to find it."

I nod.

But I don't believe him. Not really.

Asher is optimism personified. And right now, I feel like the storm cloud brewing in the distance, ready to rain down on all that positivity and push the sunshine away.

So I change the subject to something I had been thinking about before, a possible solution to one of my many problems. "Do you really want to help me?"

"Yes," Asher says, this time serious.

"Then I need you and Jade to leave."

He raises an eyebrow. "Harsh."

I clench my fist, resisting the urge to smack him again. "Not like that."

I sigh, glancing back down toward my father. As though sensing my gaze, he begins to writhe beneath the blankets, shivering from the cold yet sweating from the heat. My hand reaches for his cheek immediately, trying to comfort him, yet knowing it won't help. "I'm not an idiot," I confess. And for once, Asher holds back his witty commentary. "I know my magic isn't enough to save my father's life. I know it's useless to keep trying the same herbal remedies over and over again, and to think somehow, maybe next time, it might work. But I can't just sit back and watch him die. He's my father. I love him. I have to try. I can't give up on him."

"I know," Asher whispers. "When you love someone, it's impossible to let go. Even when they don't deserve it."

"But he does deserve it," I urge. My eyes start to sting as I look into my father's hollow expression, into those lids that still haven't opened. What I wouldn't give to just speak to him again, to say these words and know he's heard them. "He loves me so much. He's done so much to keep me safe. And I never appreciated it. I never appreciated him. All he ever wanted was to be able to see me grow old, to see me free of the curse. And if I can't give him that, I want to at least let him know that I'm happy, that I'll be all right. All I want is a little more time together."

"What can I do?"

I turn to Asher. "My father won't survive another trip through the mountains. If he's still like this by the time we have to leave, he'll die before the bombs even go off. And if my magic isn't enough to save him, then there's only one other thing that might. Medicine. Earthly medicine. We still have twelve days before the general is supposed to attack. That's enough time for you to get back to the base, to steal antibiotics from the supply room, and to give them to one of the wolves to bring back here to me."

"You could come with us," Asher says, but his heart isn't in it.

I smile at him. "You know I can't."

And he does. He understands. Asher may have come here to save me, but he can't force me to leave. To abandon my father. To abandon Cole.

So he stands because we both know the conversation is over. "I'll go tell the others there's been a change of plans."

"Thanks."

But before he leaves, he looks over his shoulder. There's something simmering beneath those indigo eyes that I don't understand, something that reads my thoughts even better than I can. "I meant what I said before," Asher says softly. "Don't do anything rash. Those faerie priestesses put curses on the magic because they wanted them to be broken, because they wanted the magic to be freed. So there has to be a way. Don't give up hope."

I smile at him.

But I don't say anything.

And he mistakes my expression for agreement.

It's not.

It's appreciation.

It's gratitude.

Only when he leaves, does it fade.

My memory flashes back to the story Cole told me. What Asher said was sweet and kind, but also naïve. Not every curse was meant to be a happy ending in disguise. The faeries had just watched their entire world fall apart. They had just watched humans greedily thieve magic from all ends of the planet. They were helpless. All the creatures they were supposed to protect disappeared. Everything they loved vanished.

No.

I don't think they were feeling as benevolent as Asher thinks when they put those curses on our bloodlines.

My mind whirls back to the story of the mad king, the one with the power to control the weather but the curse of losing his mind, the one who murdered his entire family because of the faerie's spell.

Not all curses were meant to be broken.

Some were just meant to hurt.

Some were just meant to convince us that magic wasn't worth the pain of life, that dying was the only escape, that sometimes sacrifice is the only way out.

My father moans.

I lean over him. "I'm here," I murmur. "I'm right here."

But in the back of my mind, a new idea lingers.

One I'm not sure I'm brave enough to face.

Twenty-Two

Asher and Jade leave the next day, taking two of the wolves with them. Cole and I stand at the door for a long time, watching them slowly disappear into the distance. With every step they take, my mind wanders closer and closer to the conversation with Asher, to the idea he brought to life in the back edge of my mind, the one I know he never meant to put there. If I'm being honest with myself, it's been there for a while. Lingering in the background, waiting for me to finally find the courage to face it.

But now isn't that time.

Not yet.

Not when there is still so much left to do.

"I actually think I might miss them," Cole murmurs, pulling me closer against his chest. His hands are clasped in front of my waist, and I fold my fingers around them, leaning my head back and closing my eyes, just breathing this moment in.

"Then again," he continues softly, placing his lips at the base of my neck and sending a shiver right through me. "I think we do just fine on our own."

"Mhmm," I sigh, unable to speak as he trails light kisses along my skin.

"So," he whispers, breath tickling the sensitive spot below my ear. He continues to nibble, fluttering my nerves, making my heartbeat run wild. "That whole engagement thing is over, right?"

"Oh, I don't know," I comment lightly, grinning.

He growls softly.

"I think—" I pause, gasping as his tongue flicks against my skin, burning so hot I think I might just melt to the ground.

"What was that?"

"I said..." The words come out airy and barely audible, so I clear my throat as Cole laughs softly into my ear. "Oh, never mind."

I surrender, spinning his arms so we face each other and reaching my hands over his broad shoulders. Those gray eyes sparkle with blue highlights, and a self-satisfied smirk dances along Cole's lips. But there's something sensitive in his expression too, something honest and unsure. So I lift my fingers, playing with the hairs at the base of his neck in a way that makes him tremble, and with my other hand, I lightly trace those scars across his temple. When I touch them, he doesn't flinch the way he once did. He doesn't freeze up and close himself off. Instead, his mask falls, revealing the lonely man hiding beneath the bravado, the one I want more than anything to save.

"The engagement is most definitely off," I whisper.

The instant the words are out, a smile passes over his lips, spreading an inner light to his entire face. Joy. Just pure, unadulterated bliss. The sort I know he won't be able to contain because he's a beast, and that's my favorite thing about him. He's wild and untamed and free. He's powerful and fierce, filled with raw, untapped energy. And when he feels, he does it with everything he has. He doesn't know how to hold back.

Which is why I'm not at all surprised when his hands grip my waist, and my feet suddenly fly off the ground. I'm giggling because his happiness is so infectious that it wraps me up in a glow so bright there's no escaping it. I'm bundled in him and his joy, free for a moment from all the weight that holds me down, because Cole is strong enough to lift me and spin me and make all those burdens fly away.

The moment ends too soon.

My toes barely touch the floor, but already, the weight of the world drags me back down to reality. Cole's stormy eyes are still lit with lightning fire, but my roots have buried deep. I'm grounded.

One by one, the burdens all come back.

My father.

My magic.

My curse.

The faerie woman.

The bombs.

The ticking clock, winding down, reminding me that time is still running out whether I want it to or not.

"Come on," I say with a sigh, stepping back. "There's a lot we have to do."

Cole doesn't let go. His fingers tighten around my waist, as though he wants to hold on to this brief reprieve for a little while longer. But we both know the moment has passed. With a deep exhale, he loosens his grip and runs his hands through his already disheveled black hair.

"Eleven days," he snarls, but I know the frustration he's releasing isn't directed at me. "Where do we even begin?"

I don't know how to answer him. The sheer amount of work is staggering. Not only do we need to figure out the bare basics, how to bring food, how to bring shelter, how to move everyone to the new location he and Jade scouted out. We also need to figure out how to move my father, if it's safe to move the faerie woman, what to do with all of the research we've been reading about the magic. Every time I think of one solution, another question pops up, another obstacle to face.

"I guess we just," I pause, shrugging. "I don't know. Take it one step at a time."

And that's exactly what we do.

One task at a time. One solution at a time.

One, then the next, then another.

On the first day, we focus on food. For hours, we stand in the greenhouse, plucking tomatoes off vines, digging herbs from the ground, pulling potatoes from the dirt. Anything and everything we can get our hands on is packed away into baskets. And as soon as one section is cleared, I use my magic to grow more, repeating the process over and over again until I'm so exhausted I can't even stand. Cole catches me before I fall, angry when he realizes how much of a toll I allowed the power to take. Even as I protest, he carries me up to my room, bundling me beneath the blankets on my bed and telling me to rest.

The next day, I'm ready to work again, but when I reach the kitchen, I find the greenhouse and all the gardens within have been torn apart. Cole doesn't say anything, he just leads me away to another room, giving me another problem to solve. Shelter. For Cole, for his people, living in the mountains will be second nature. Wolves and bears don't need cover from the cold, they don't need food, they don't need cloaks or fires or warmth. I'm the weak link. So we spend the afternoon and the evening bundling up blankets and warm clothes, a makeshift tent for me to sleep beneath, and dry sticks for fires. Every time I glance at Cole, his brows are pulled together, and worry lines are etched across his face. I know what he's thinking, I'm thinking it too.

How long can I really last in the wilderness?

How long will we be able to stay together?

How long before I'm forced to go back home?

Neither of us mentions anything as dawn springs on the third day. Instead, we turn our focus to the research. The sun crosses the sky before we've even been able to make a dent sorting through the papers and books, figuring out what needs to be saved and what we can afford to lose in the bombs. On the fourth day, we finally pack everything we need into baskets. On the fifth, we choose a few of our favorite books from the library and add them to the supplies. My heart aches when I stand in the center of so much intellectual wealth, knowing in a few days, countless volumes will be buried beneath rock, perhaps never to be seen again.

When the sixth day begins, Cole is already gone from the bed we've started to share. I miss his warmth, the weight of his arms around me, how safe and secure he makes me feel. But today, he's taking the first group of shifters to the new spot in the mountains, and I know he won't be home until tomorrow. So I spend the day leaning over my father, trying not to panic, trying to soothe any pain I can. And when it becomes too tough, I take a break to walk around the castle, grabbing a few things I can't bear to let the bombs destroy. Some of the glamorous dresses from my armoire, ones I know aren't practical but need to be saved. I take the painting down in Cole's room, the one over the fireplace. He's never told me it depicts him with his parents, but I just know it does, and I know he would be heartbroken to lose it. And then I ask the snow leopard to take me to his parents' room, the place I soon realize is where I first found Cole in the form of the wolf, howling at the moon, so alone. His mother's combs still rest on her dressing table. His father's coats still hang in the closet. I take whatever I can fit and put it with all of the other supplies piled on sleds to be dragged through the snow toward our new home.

Cole returns the next day with a few of the wolves, and then they lead the rest of his people toward the mountain. By the evening of the eighth day, Cole and I are alone in an empty castle, in an empty kingdom. Just the two of us and the two people we don't know how to move.

My father.

And the faerie.

"We have two days to figure something out," Cole murmurs into my hair.

We're lying in his bed, a spot that's become my own personal haven, a spot where it feels like there is nothing we can't overcome. Our legs are entwined and my head rests on his chest, listening to the heavy thump of his heart beating. One of his arms hugs me close, latched around my small waist in a grip that says he might never let go.

To be honest, I don't want him to. I want to stay here and pretend that the sun will never rise. That tomorrow will never come. For the first time in my life, I wouldn't mind spending the rest of it in the dark.

"Do you think they'll come back with the medicine for my father? Do you think Asher managed to steal it?"

Cole runs his fingers through my hair. "We'll wait all day tomorrow for any sign of them. We don't have to leave until the next day. I just want to be out of sight before the bombs start going off."

I nod. Tomorrow will be the ninth day since Asher left. We might still be pushing it by leaving on day ten when the attack is supposed to happen on day eleven, but this is Cole's gift to me, the one I've come to realize is the most precious of all—time. Time to wait for a miracle, for the one thing that might just keep my father alive.

"And what are we going to do with her?" I ask, changing the subject. I don't want to think about my father, not now, not when it's all I've been focusing on for days.

Cole doesn't need me to clarify at all. Just like my father occupies all of my spare thoughts, the faerie occupies all of his. "I don't know," he murmurs quietly.

"I've been thinking," I tell him, twisting ever so slightly so I can stare up at his face. My hands stop caressing his chest and travel up to his cheek instead. Those churning gray eyes find mine immediately. "I don't think moving her will be a problem, because we'd be doing it to save her. The reason Asher and Jade were able to get closer than anyone else, were able to get past the wall and into the castle, I think, was because their intentions were to save me, not to harm her. Everyone else who ever came from the base was coming here to destroy the magic, to destroy her, and that's why her magic killed them. But we're moving her to protect her."

He smiles softly, but I can tell by the storm still brewing in his gaze that he's already figured that out. My words provide no comfort. His thoughts are further into the future, focused on the riddle we still haven't been able to solve—how to release his people's magic, how to wake her up and restore them.

I don't let my thoughts linger too long on that question. My gut urges me to change the subject.

"Cole?"

"Yeah?"

I want to tell him I love him.

I do.

And I've known it for a while. But in these past few days, every time I try to tell him, the words die on my tongue. My throat closes, locking them away, because when they rise to my lips, they sound too much like goodbye. Too much like a concession instead of a promise.

I don't know why.

Or maybe I do. But I'm just not ready to admit it.

"Thank you," I whisper instead.

"You don't have to—"

But I place my finger over his lips, stopping him.

He nips at me.

And I realize I've inadvertently awoken my beast.

"Cole!" I shriek, but it's too late. He's already rolled over, pinning me beneath him, weight heavy enough to keep me from moving, but I know it takes all of his strength to not crush me. His muscles are flexed, holding him over me, and with a low growl, he buries his face in my neck, kissing me until I'm giggling and laughing and filling the air around with happiness instead of sorrow. And when his kisses grow deeper, the mood shifts again, and I know the time for talking is over.

Hours later, the sun blinds me painfully. I roll away, turning in Cole's arms, grumbling. I'm not ready for the harsh light of day, not ready to face a new dawn. But even in my sleepy mind, a thought stops me.

Haven't those curtains been closed for days? Haven't—

Thunder silences my question.

The ground beneath us trembles.

An earthquake.

That same nightmare all over again.

"Cole!" I scream, shaking him awake.

For a moment the earth stills. And then again, my world shudders. And I realize, it's not another earthquake.

It's the bombs.

Two days too soon.

Twenty-Three

We're both awake in an instant, leaping from the warmth of the bed into the cool morning air, shocking any lingering sluggishness away.

The ground shifts.

I lose my footing, slipping sideways, stumbling on uneasy feet until Cole's hands wrap around my waist, steadying me. I latch on to him as though he's my anchor in this storm.

"My father!" I shriek, trying to be heard over the deafening roar of rock splitting apart.

"Go," Cole orders. "I'll get your father. I'll get the faerie. Just start running beyond the wall, start running toward the mountains, and we'll catch up to you."

"No!" I shout, shaking my head. I've spent my life running. I need to help. I need to do something. And then I get an idea. "I think I can buy us some time. Go. I'll meet you outside the front gate as soon as I can."

"Omorose—"

But I cut him off with a kiss.

I know he won't want me in harm's way, but I can't just run. I can't just save myself and abandon him. I have magic. I have power. I have strength. And I can fight to keep us both alive. There's no way Cole will be able to move fast enough to get my father and the faerie into sleds, no way he can pull them both to safety before the mountain crumbles. We need more time. And I think I know how to get it.

Before he can mutter a protest, I tear our lips apart and sprint from his room. My father's life is in Cole's hands now, and I know there is no safer place for it to be, especially if I can keep the city afloat for just a little while longer.

The magic surges to my fingertips before I'm even outside. My mind is already diving deep, connected to the soil and rock, sinking down the side of that cliff, searching for any plants and any roots I can utilize. While my feet continue to pound against stone, leading themselves forward, my thoughts are on the mountain.

Grow.

Right now, that simple command is the only thing that matters.

Grow.

Every plant within the range of my power listens. Roots elongate, wrapping around stone, across cracks, over and under and through in an intricate underground web. Ivy drops over the city wall, twisting and turning, expanding over the cliff face, crisscrossing into a net.

Another blast explodes.

The ground trembles.

But it steadies. It holds.

Wrapped up in the power, I feel the vines expand and contract, fighting the pressure of the boulders that want to break free, but the net holds. For now.

I blink away the magic, using my eyes to see, and realize I'm standing at the edge of the earth. Fear freezes me, clenching all my muscles, shocking my system. Sky stretches endlessly before me, and the ground is far, far below, clouded by a morning haze. My cloak whips with the ferocious breeze, flapping loudly. Coarse rocks cut into my palms, and I realize I'm on the city wall, gripping the stones to keep my balance as I stand over the edge of the cliff.

When the magic took control, I let my feet lead me.

Why did they have to lead me here?

Another detonation shakes the ground. Hundreds of feet below, a bulbous orange glow angrily stretches into the air. Smoky tendrils stretch for me, reaching up to the vantage point where I stand, trying to pull me under.

An electric fire pulses up my chest, a scream I can't unleash, and my heartbeat runs rapid. My lips begin to quiver. My hands too. Every single nerve in my body wants to run, to hide, to cower in terror.

I've never been afraid of heights.

But then again, until this moment, I've never been faced with the very real possibility of plunging to my death.

Be brave.

The thought pushes through the fear.

My mother's voice. The exact thing I needed to hear.

With a deep breath, I charge headfirst back into my magic, wrapping it around me and shrugging off the stifling alarm. My focus returns to the ivy and to the roots, stretched so far they're about to snap.

I grow more.

I am the earth.

I am nature.

Every time the mountain starts to slip away, dropping one inch, then another, I hold tighter to my power, fusing the vines through the cracks, holding every bit of rock that tries to drop away. I'm stronger than the bombs. I keep together what they break apart. For a moment, I truly feel invincible.

And then heat burns, flaring over my senses.

I scream, crying out as pain tears through me.

My hold on the magic vanishes as fire scalds my skin, yanking me back to reality. I rub at my arms, trying to push the flames away, but when I blink, the sky above me is blue. The stone beneath me is cold. The hurt is gone.

My heart sinks. I rise from my spot on the floor and peer over the edge.

The cliff has become a wall of fire. All the plants I've grown are little more than tinder, feeding the flames. Already, the ground shifts the slightest bit more.

But it's enough.

I don't need my magic to know the vines are burning away, the ivy is shriveling, the roots are tearing apart.

The mountain is going to fall.

And it's going to take me with it.

"Omorose!" Cole shouts.

He's far away, running across the city wall. Before I can blink, he shifts into the black bear, charging toward me on all fours.

I try to run to him.

But the earth shakes and I fall, tripping over my own feet.

When I slam against stone, a different power takes hold. Lava courses beneath my skin, lava followed by glaciers that bury the heat, replacing it with a deep freeze. My body seizes as the mix of fire and ice rakes through me. The world disappears for a moment as I fall helplessly into the dark core of my soul where the rose waits. Petals peel away, more than I've ever lost before. And for the first time, the bud looks frail and fragile. The bloom is no longer bright red with life, but a deeper maroon, rotting at the edges. My magic is taking payment. The curse is shredding time away, ripping it forcefully from me. And there is absolutely nothing I can do.

A wet nose rubs my forehead, rousing me.

He growls softly, a sound of worry and concern.

"Cole?" I murmur, reaching blindly.

My fingers brush against velvet fur and latch on as he sinks down next to me. Every ounce of strength I have goes into lifting my aching body from the stone and rolling onto Cole's back, hugging my arms around his neck.

And then we run.

Cole's muscles coil and flex beneath me as he carries us both to safety. Huddled against his warmth, I gradually return to myself. The curse falls away. The magic falls away. I breathe in the woodsy, wild scent of Cole, knowing everything will be okay because I'm with him, we're together, so nothing can go wrong. Then my eyes fall open, landing on the one thing I never thought I would see.

The faerie woman.

In the middle of the main street.

Discarded.

"Cole!" I shout, gripping tighter.

But he doesn't respond, doesn't slow his movements or growl or do anything.

"Cole!" I try again, thinking he didn't hear. "We have to get her. We have to save her. We don't know what will happen."

But then he roars.

A deep, torn sound.

And I know.

He left her to come find me. He knew exactly what would happen. He knew exactly what he was giving up.

I turn, peering over my shoulder.

The city has started to vanish. The ground slopes down behind us, cracking and fissuring, as dust begins to fill the air. A snap shatters the sky, and my eyes flick to the castle. The stones have broken in half. I get the briefest flicker of gold as the ballroom twists into view. Sunlight glimmers off the chandeliers, and then the building sinks, slipping farther and farther back, dropping away. Just like that, the only home I've known in the past ten years disappears, falling out of sight, soon to be a pile of rubble on the ground far below.

The mountain trembles so violently that my teeth begin to chatter as we run.

Cole slips, but he doesn't fall.

Only his instincts keep us alive.

Every time I glance behind, more of the land has disappeared. We run and run, but not fast enough. The edge of the cliff is creeping closer. And when I glance back to the faerie woman, she is no longer resting peacefully. The sled holding her is sloped, slipping backward, sliding closer and closer to oblivion, taking any chance Cole has at reuniting with his people with her.

I lose sight of her golden glow when we reach the front gate of the city. Cole leaps from the wall, not even glancing behind, focusing only on the open wilderness ahead. Without pause, he clasps his jaw around the rope attached to my father's sled, dragging us both away from the growing precipice as fast as he can.

"Cole!" I shout, trying to make him stop.

But he's a bear.

And I'm a girl.

Not really a fair fight.

Suddenly, I understand what Asher was talking about all those days ago. About sacrifice. About how sometimes the people being sacrificed for might not want to live with the guilt of what was lost.

I can't.

I won't be the reason Cole loses everyone he loves.

A whole race of people.

An entire kingdom of innocent lives.

I won't let him make that sacrifice.

So I dive back into my magic, biting my lip so hard that I bleed, ignoring the metallic taste rolling over my tongue. The curse has depleted my strength. I'm spent. And reaching for my magic is like tugging on a locked door, futile. Still, I yank and pull with all my might until my fingertips start to tingle with power. And it hurts. My body is so weak that even just touching my magic has ignited the curse. My heart burns as more time is ripped away before I've even done anything. But I clench my muscles, fighting the pain, and reach out with my other senses.

I feel her immediately.

The magic calls to me, and I respond, wrapping her in vines, coiling them around the sled, and then sending them toward me.

"Cole," I whisper, trying to get his attention.

This time, I really think he doesn't hear. I can barely hear myself.

So I do the next best thing, I let go of his fur and fall, landing hard against the snow. That pain is nothing compared to the torment of the curse rolling through me. Cole stops immediately, turning toward me with those smoky gray eyes, more mournful than I've ever seen them.

"Pull," I cough hoarsely.

I can see he doesn't understand what I'm trying to say.

Using more magic, I wrap the vines around his paws, struggling for words as the power and the curse rip through me, euphoric and excruciating all at once.

His eyes go wide.

He lets go of the rope connected to my father's sled and sinks his teeth into the vines. He pulls.

The magic vanishes as the final ounces of my strength give out, and I collapse against the frozen land. At the edges of my vision, I see the faerie. The ground to either side of her is gone, and I know her magic is the only thing keeping her escape route intact, as though it knows we're doing everything we can to save her. The last remnants of the city wall crumble. Slate roofs all around her drop away. The front gate falls sideways, crashing against the ground and rolling back before disappearing over the edge.

Cole yanks.

The sled moves closer. And with each inch of ground gained, the empty road behind her drops away.

A boom splits the air, the sound of the city shattering against the ground far, far below. A cloud of ash and dust erupts, shrouding the faerie in darkness.

For a moment, the earth stops.

There are no sounds.

The mountains are still, silent.

Rocky particles glimmer like ashen snowfall, almost beautiful.

And then a dull, golden light shines through the shadows, too low to be the sun. Cole grunts, but he doesn't stop until the sled is right next to my father's, using his claws to slash through the vines my magic created.

The faerie woman is peacefully asleep.

Unchanged. Unaffected.

Cole collapses, discarding the form of the bear and landing on his knees, head bowed to the floor as his fists clench tight in an emotion I don't know how to read. Relief I think. Overwhelming relief.

"Cole," I murmur, trying to find my voice. "You…you risked everything."

He looks up, capturing me with his fierce gaze, charged with lightning fire. "Omorose, you are everything," he confesses softly. I breathe in deep as those words steal all the breath from my chest. "I'd do anything to keep you safe."

I don't know what to do as he crawls closer, pulling me into his arms, burying his head into my neck, breathing in my scent. I want to throw my arms around him. I want to kiss him, to hold him, to tell him I love him.

But I'm frozen.

You are everything.

I'd do anything to keep you safe.

Everything.

Anything.

Suddenly, I'm nauseous.

Cole risked everything to be with me. He'd do anything to keep me safe. Because he doesn't know. Because I never told him.

He thinks I'm his forever.

And I wanted so badly for that to be true.

I wanted so badly to be his forever.

But time is my curse. Time is the one thing I can't give him.

I'm going to die. The magic is going to kill me. He's going to be alone, and I'm going to leave him broken and crushed.

Unless...

The idea I'd been pushing away flies to the surface, no longer able to be ignored. I've known for a while how this would end, ever since I first touched that faerie and felt her magic pull me under. I wasn't ready to face it then, but now, I am. Knowing that Cole loves me, that he was ready to give up everything for me, makes me want to do the same for him. So I open my heart and my soul and let the truth wash over me.

I know how to get rid of my magic.

I know how to awaken the faerie.

My curse is too strong to break. All I can do is surrender and be satisfied with knowing I won't be leaving Cole alone, that my sacrifice won't be in vain.

My death will make all of his dreams come true.

Twenty-Four

I wait until Cole is fast asleep before I roll free of his arms, leaning up on my elbow to look down over his face, peaceful in slumber.

This is going to be the hardest part.

Saying goodbye.

As I brush my fingers through his wonderfully unruly ebony hair, I try to find comfort in knowing this is the only way. This is how it was always supposed to end. If the general was willing to bring down a mountain, risking who knows how many innocent lives, then he'll never stop coming after the magic—after the faerie or after me. I'll never be free.

But Cole, he has a chance. I can give him that chance. If the magic is gone, the general and everyone at the base will think they've won. With the magic free, Cole and his people can pretend to be innocent humans caught in the crossfire. Or they can flee to the mountains and remain as they are now, a kingdom of animals in the wild. The point is they will have a choice, they will have each other, and they will have freedom.

"Cole," I murmur, not sure where to begin. There are so many things I want to say, and yet, nothing sounds right. "You made me feel alive for the first time in my life. In a world where I felt so impossibly trapped, you gave me a taste of freedom, and I can never thank you enough for that. And I know this isn't how you want it to end, and I wish so much that things could be different, that I could be different for you, but I guess that's not how life goes sometimes. I hope you know that no matter what happens, I'll always be with you, and you'll always be with me. In that small way, we can still have our slice of forever."

He sighs, turning toward me. A smile passes over his lips.

It breaks my heart.

"Please forgive me," I whisper, bringing my palm to his cheek. And then I lean down, kissing him softly, missing the silky touch of his lips the instant I pull away. And because it's my last chance, I say the three words I've been too afraid to say, the ones I somehow knew would always mean goodbye. "I love you."

Then I force myself to look away.

I force myself to crawl quietly toward the front of the tent, easing one flap aside, leaving the warmth and entering the cold, dark night.

Animals rest peacefully on the snow all around me, not at all fazed by the damp, frozen ground. We only got here a little while ago. Cole spent hours pulling my father, the faerie, and me through the mountains toward the spot where his people were waiting for us. All the effort it took is the only reason he's sleeping so soundly now, the only reason I had any hope of escaping his embrace without waking him up.

Eyes watch me as I cross over the open field, feet crunching on the ice. The wolves stationed themselves outside of our tent, keeping guard over their king. But they don't try to stop me. They have no reason to—they don't know enough.

I visit my father first.

He's alive. Barely.

My presence soothes him, as though he can somehow sense I'm near. He mumbles softly, nonsense, and shifts his face toward me, nudging the pillow. Just in case he can hear me, I don't say anything as I wipe the sweat from his brow and tuck the blankets in closer. I don't want him to know this is goodbye. I want him to think it's just another visit, one of many to come. I want him to stay lost in his imagination, to stay wrapped up in the only happy ending he'll ever find. The medicine Asher was supposed to send never arrived. But maybe it's better this way. Maybe it's better if my father slips peacefully away, never knowing all of his dreams for me didn't have a chance to come true.

After a few more silent moments, I slip back into the night.

One of the wolves is standing right outside the tent when I emerge, watching me with a cocked head, eyes piercing through the darkness.

"Go back to sleep," I urge.

But he doesn't.

He follows me as I step quietly toward the faerie's tent, eyes boring into my side like a physical weight.

"Go to sleep," I order again.

But he just continues to stare.

Stubborn.

Everyone in this entire kingdom is so frustratingly stubborn.

But I can't risk him waking Cole. So I take a step closer, putting my hand out. He steps into my palm, allowing me to scratch behind his ears. And then he flops over onto his back, rolling his tongue out to the side like a puppy searching for a belly rub. Such a softy.

"Not now," I chide. He whines. "Cole asked me to check on her."

At that, his ears perk up, and he straightens.

"That's right," I continue, keeping my voice even and low. "Your king is trying to get some much-needed rest after dragging me all the way here, so go back to sleep and don't disturb him."

His head cocks, perceptive.

I wonder if he can taste the lie in the air? Or do my human instincts give me away? Can he hear my blood pounding in my ears? Can he smell the salty sweat on my palms? Can he sense my fear?

I'll never know.

He stays where he is but drops his head down to his paws and closes his eyes, giving me the privacy I asked for. And that will have to do, because the moon is rising higher overhead, shining a silver light over the mountains, reminding me that it's only a matter of time before Cole wakes and realizes I'm gone. It won't take him long to find me.

I slip silently into the faerie's tent.

The golden glow blinds me.

I blink a few times, allowing my eyes to adjust.

There she is. Same as always. Blond hair in perfect disarray. Skin shimmering with an inner glow. Features fluid, yet always stunning. Magic radiating out, almost tangible. The events of the day haven't touched her.

What does she see behind those closed eyes?

What dreams does she live in?

What nightmares?

I take a step closer, feeling the magnetic pull of her power wrapping around me, recognizing me for what I am—the only thing that can save her. I should have realized it a long time ago, the first time I ever felt that mesmerizing lure of her magic. And maybe I did.

But now, standing over her, I can't deny it.

She's a faerie. She's a flower.

She's dying. She's been dying. It's the only explanation for why she stole the magic from Cole's people. She needed it to heal herself and to be protected while the spell ran its course, however long that might be.

But I'm here now. And I can give her life the same way I give all nature life—by giving up my own.

As I sit by her side, my fingers tremble. My eyes start to burn. There's only an inch of air between our fingers, but the small space is filled with vast meaning. I can't close the distance.

Am I ready to say goodbye? Am I ready to die?

I close my eyes, pulling my hand into a fist, stilled by doubt, letting my imagination take over. In my mind's eye, I see Cole reunited with his people in a bustling new home filled with humans and animals alike. I see them free, no longer pursued, no longer hunted. Children shift from pups to toddlers in the bright light of day, not afraid. I see the man I love smiling and laughing openly, his cloudy eyes have cleared, and somewhere deep within them there's a memory of me that he holds close to his heart.

And I see myself back in a place I never thought I would find again. Home. With my mother and my sister, with all the people we left behind. Eventually my father will find us too, and in that beautiful afterlife, we'll be a family again.

I hold on to those dreams as I uncurl my fingers.

Maybe, for once, my hopes can come true. Maybe the curse has been the answer all along. Maybe in death I'll finally be free.

I sense the heat of her skin before I touch it, pausing.

Be brave.

A voice whispers.

Be brave.

And for the first time, I realize, that voice is me. Not my mother. Not my sister. Not my younger self.

But me. The woman I've become.

Strong. Brave.

And ready to face whatever comes next.

I close the distance.

Our hands clasp tight, and the faerie pulls me under. I don't resist. I surrender to the magic. I let hers overtake me, and I open my soul, freely giving away every ounce of power within. My sense of self vanishes. I'm no longer Omorose. I'm pure, untainted energy. And I disappear within the faerie, zipping straight for her heart, realizing for the first time how rotten it is.

Grow.

Heal.

Live.

Three thoughts are all I have left. And just like a flower, the faerie blooms beneath the force of those commands. The mildew staining her soul disappears. The rancid decay destroying her from the inside out retreats, slips away. Her body is like a tree that has decomposed under the passage of time and I'm reviving it, digging the roots down deep, stretching the leaves to the sky, pushing the slow assault of death away.

And then my pain strikes.

We switch places.

The flower at the center of my soul wilts. The rosy hue turns darker, rotting at the edges. The petals widen, drooping away from the core, peeling off one by one.

I couldn't stop even if I wanted to.

I'm too lost in the power and the pain.

The faerie pulls on my magic more and more, growing stronger with every second that I grow weaker, yanking my life away and burying it within her. My strength gives out. I collapse against her.

Distantly, I feel arms shake me.

But I'm drowning.

Words are shouted. They don't reach me.

I'm slipping away, drifting deeper.

The end is near.

The golden aura of the faerie surrounds me, burning so bright I can't escape the heat. My flower shrivels. The rose, my namesake, is disappearing. There are only a few petals left.

Five.

Then four.

A fist clenches my heart, wrapping tightly around the bloom, stealing all my breath away. I'm suffocating. And then that hand pulls, twists, yanks, doing whatever it can to leech every last bit of magic I have.

Three.

The pressure mounts until I'm torn down the middle.

Two.

I can't fight anymore. I'm about to shatter. To break.

We snap apart.

I fly back, catapulting into the real world, landing in arms I knew would be there to catch me.

"Omorose!" Cole shouts as he cradles me to his chest.

I barely have the strength to keep my eyes open.

His warm palm caresses my cheek, and looking down with eyes as tumultuous as a thunderstorm, he whispers, "What did you do?"

I want to answer him.

I want to explain.

But my tongue is heavy. My lips won't open.

"She saved my life," a voice answers slowly.

I smile because I know who that voice belongs to, even if I can't find the energy to turn my head and look upon her. The faerie. Awake. Alive.

And with that small validation that my sacrifice won't be for naught, my soul lets go.

The curse takes its final toll.

The last petal falls.

Twenty-Five

I thought death would be swift and quick. But it's not.

It's painfully, achingly slow.

My eyes slip closed, surrounding me in darkness. A wave of cold travels slowly up my skin, starting at my fingertips and toes, creeping ever closer to my heart.

I can't move.

Can't speak.

I'm paralyzed, trapped in a world of shadow.

But I can hear. And that's what hurts the most.

"Do something! Help her!" Cole shouts.

I want to wince but I can't. He still doesn't know what's happening. He still thinks he can save me. Because he trusts me. He trusts that I always told him the truth.

"There's nothing I can do." The voice is cold and unkind, almost aggressive. It doesn't match the beautiful face I remember. "Besides," the faerie continues, "I wouldn't help a human thief even if I could."

Cole snarls and his muscles clench tight. His arms tremble beneath me, anger growing uncontrollable. It's always been an easier emotion for him to handle than despair. He's escaping into the rage, trying to lose himself within it. "You're no better," he sneers. "You stole everything from me. Everything."

"That wasn't personal," she snips, and then sighs. Her voice grows softer for a moment. "And this isn't either. There really is nothing I can do. I'm not strong enough to break her curse, not by myself."

Cole stills. "What curse? Her curse is pain."

The faerie laughs, a quiet smug sound, as though she expects no better than a lie from a human, from someone like me.

I want to hit her. I want to hug him. I want to wake up and apologize. Anything but this horribly passive participation.

"Dear prince," the faerie continues, "her curse is death."

"No," Cole whispers. His arms tighten around me, crushing me against his chest. "No!" he roars, anguish palpable in the way the word rips from his throat, raw and torn. "There has to be something, some way, some..."

I lay limp in his arms as he trails off.

He shifts. And even though I can't see, I know his eyes are on me. His fingers brush against my cheek, ever so softly, reminding me of that first night so long ago when he was little more than an unknown stranger giving me hope that I might find somewhere I belonged. And in his arms, I did.

"Please," Cole begs. "Please don't leave me."

His voice in that moment is the most brutal sound I've ever heard.

And it's the last.

My ears film over, and I'm left with the haunting echo of Cole's hopeless plea, until everything fades away. All my senses vanish. I no longer feel his arms around me, no longer hear his heart thumping in my chest. He's gone. I'm gone.

Is this death?

This endless night?

Will I just drift in this oblivion forever?

My awareness shifts.

Bright lights spark in the distance, like stars twinkling in the faraway sky. And then they widen, they grow. My body is weightless and I'm floating, flying higher and higher.

Suddenly the room pops back into view.

But I'm no longer Omorose.

She is below me, deathly pale in Cole's arms as he sways back and forth on his knees, clasping her tight, burying his face in her neck. The faerie stands over them both, expression hard, yet her eyes glisten with sympathy.

Am I a ghost?

A lingering spirit?

Before the answer comes, something grabs hold of me, a force that wants to yank me away.

I'm defenseless against the pull.

I soar backward, until I'm outside of the tent looking down at an open field lit only by the glow of the moon. I lift higher, until I can see every animal and every tree and every snow patch in the valley. A glimmer of golden light catches my attention in the distance.

But the mysterious force tugs strongly, and I'm whisked away on the wind, blown by a strong breeze, moving faster and faster with each passing second, until tall peaks and low dales blur into a carpet of black and white shadows. The ground speeds by, giving way to boundless plains, expansive forests, and rivers that flicker in and out of view. I shoot across an endless sea that sparkles with starlight, and only when I see a dark patch of land in the distance do I begin to slow.

I have no idea where I am.

Why I'm here.

A city larger than anything I ever knew existed slips into view, alive with energy as lights pierce the night, bright against the darkness.

Electricity. An impossible amount.

Buildings stretch out before me, and I sink, dropping closer to the winding streets, arriving at my unknown destination—a large brick structure looking more like a castle than a home.

I slip inside, drifting right through the closed wooden door, down an entrance hallway, across a giant ballroom lined with beds. Children sleep beneath the covers, eyes closed, faces peaceful if dirty and unclean. I fly over them through another door.

Then I pause.

The force pulling on me stops.

At the end of the room, a girl sits close to a crackling fire, face buried in the pages of a book. Rags hang off her thin frame and hole-ridden socks cover her feet, offering a glimpse of soot-stained toes. Beneath the grime, her skin is a rich bronze. Her messy hair shines with the glow of the fire, a deep chestnut brown.

There's something so familiar.

I drift closer.

As though sensing me, she looks up.

And everything becomes clear.

No!

I want to shout.

No!

Because beneath the cinders spotting her cheeks, her face is my face. And those green eyes curiously glancing around the room are golden at the core, just like the sun on a spring day, just like my mother's eyes used to be.

I know why I'm here.

The curse.

Even in death I can't escape it.

My spirit lingers with the magic, and the curse brought us here, to the heir I didn't realize was somehow still alive.

My sister.

My innocent little sister.

Her blood is my blood—the last of my lineage.

I try to push against the curse, to turn around and run away, but the hold is unbreakable, and I drift closer to her, agonizingly slow.

She looks exactly how I imagined.

Just like Papa. Except for her eyes.

I drink her in, amazed by how mature she seems, how much older than the little two-year-old I left behind. What has her life been like these past ten years? How did she find her way here, to a land across the sea, so far out of reach?

I'm right in front of her.

And then the magic brushes against her skin.

Those green eyes widen. The book falls from her hands.

Her brows come together.

"Ro Ro?" she whispers.

My old nickname.

Before she has time to say anything, the magic latches on to her heart, tearing into her skin. She cries out, falling to the cold ground. I try to stop it, to twist and yank, to keep my hold on the magic, but it slips through my invisible fingers like water, unstoppable.

Her small body trembles.

I want to hold her because I remember the day not so long ago that I felt the magic burn my soul for the first time. I'd never felt pain like that before. I want to tell her everything will be all right, even though I know it won't. I want to comfort her. Most of all, I want to tell her the same thing my father told me so long ago.

Don't use it.

No matter how hard the magic is to resist, live.

Don't give your years away.

Don't let the curse own you.

But I can't say any of those things because as the magic sinks beneath her skin, the world fades. The light of the fire dims and my awareness recedes.

I use these last few seconds of my life to memorize every curve of her face, to silently apologize for never finding her. My deepest regret will be that I stopped looking. Because if I had known, I never would have condemned her to my fate.

But now, there's nothing I can do.

The curse binds to her soul.

My sight goes black.

And I disappear into nothing.

Twenty-Six

Electric fire zaps my chest.

Am I in hell?

The pain strikes again, burning through me.

And then there's pressure on my chest. One. Two. Three. As though someone is dropping boulders on my heart, trying to crush me. Cool air blows through my lips, filling me up. Then the pounding weight returns.

I must be in hell.

Until right now, I never believed in those Earthly gods. But where else could this place be?

Trapped in the dark, being poked and prodded by shadows, a cycle of never-ending pain. For the first time, eternity stretches before me. The curse is gone. And yet, I want it back because I can't spend the rest of my afterlife like this.

"Come on," a voice urges.

The electric fire is back.

All of a sudden, my mouth opens, sucking in a long, excruciating breath. Every inch of me prickles, stinging back to life. I start to cough, choking on air, as my lungs blaze with heat. Tears spring to my eyes, and I try to blink them away. My vision is blurred and confused.

Is that Asher above me?

What is he doing here?

Did he die too?

"Omorose!" a voice shouts.

Another head comes into view, pale skin and smoky gray eyes, a face I would recognize anywhere. Cole. And he's grinning so widely.

Maybe I'm in heaven after all.

My arms are too heavy, they won't lift. But he bends down closer, filling my entire field of view as his fingers run through my hair, and his lips sprinkle kisses all over my face.

Now, this is the sort of eternity I could get used to.

I stop struggling to move, to see, and instead just bask in his touch, sighing softly. Time can just go on and on as far as I'm concerned. I never want this to end.

Cole pulls away. I grumble in protest.

He laughs, and the beauty in that easy sound makes me shiver with pleasure. "Omorose, it's time to wake up."

When I hear that bossy command, I realize something. If this were a dream, the stubborn bear king wouldn't be taking over. Cole's lips would still be pressed against mine, they wouldn't be far away and demanding.

I blink.

The room gradually comes into view.

I blink again.

Cole kneels over me, but so does Asher and so does Jade. No offense to them, but in my dreams, Cole and I are normally alone, doing things I don't really want other people to see. Which means maybe I'm not dreaming.

Maybe...

"Am I dead?"

Asher snorts, but my eyes are on Cole.

He brushes his palm through my hair, gazing at me like I'm everything. "No," he murmurs. "You're very much alive."

My brows come together. This can't be real.

Can it?

And then Cole grins. "You're stuck with me, Omorose Bouchene. Did you really think I'd let a little thing like a curse take you away?"

I don't answer.

I just grab the back of his neck with my hands, yanking Cole down and smashing my face against his, catching my beast off-guard. He loses his balance, falling on top of me, crushing me with his weight. But there's no better pain in the world than that. And I should know, I've experienced my fair share.

Someone coughs.

I ignore it.

For the first time, happily ever after sounds like a very real possibility. My heart has swelled so wide I actually think it might burst, and I'm not really in the mood for interruptions. Most of my life has been tainted with a fear of what other people might think, and right now, I couldn't care less. Let them watch. And let them wait. Because I'm kissing Cole, and I'm going to take my time.

"Ahem," a deep voice coughs a little louder.

Nope.

Sorry.

Not happening.

But Cole has other plans. He's laughing against my lips as he reaches back and unlatches my fingers from around his neck. Deep in his eyes, the hungry beast still watches me, but the human king has regained control.

I take a long breath and glare at Asher.

A moment later, Jade punches him in the upper arm.

"Ow." He flinches, gripping the newly sore spot on his bicep and turning to her. "What was that for?"

Jade shrugs. "I recognized that look in Omorose's eyes, just figured I would help her out."

"I'm not sure I like what's happening here," he murmurs.

I grin and sit up, crossing my arms. "Well, I do."

Asher glances at me, raising his brows. "I just saved your life, you know. I think a gushing thank you is more appropriate."

That stops me, bringing a blush to my cheeks as I bite my bottom lip. "Sorry," I murmur. And with the euphoria gone, it all comes rushing back. The curse. The magic. The void. And worst of all, my sister. My eyes go wide. "But I did die. I know I did. How did you bring me back to life?"

"With a handy little thing I like to call electricity," Asher says, very proud of himself, holding up some contraption I don't recognize.

Cole reaches over, gripping my hand. His voice, I notice, isn't quite as cheerful, as though the memory still haunts him. "Your heart stopped." He swallows and his fingers tighten just a little, just enough to let me know how truly terrified he was of losing me. "You were dead. I couldn't feel a pulse, couldn't hear a beat in your chest."

He looks to Asher, at a loss for words.

"When we left last week, I couldn't help but notice that you had a bit of a noble, selfless sort of air about you," Asher says, wrinkling his nose. "I hate those sort of airs, they always mean trouble. I knew you were going to do something idiotic, just like I'd seen another person do in the past..."

He glances pointedly at Jade.

She raises one eyebrow, not backing down.

The corners of his lip twitch, revealing just how much he loves pushing her buttons. "Anyway," he continues, "we were going to send the wolves back alone with the medicine for your father, but something in both of our guts urged us to see it through. So I grabbed an emergency medical kit to bring with us, something a friend of ours back home who's training to be a doctor taught us how to use. A little CPR, a little shock from the portable defibrillator, and here we are."

He gestures nonchalantly, but I know it had to have been more difficult than that, especially when he catches my eye. Worry lines still flicker deep in his indigo irises, flashes of lavender concern.

"Thank you," I tell him, putting every ounce of gratitude I can into those two words. Then I turn to Jade. "Thank you both for saving my life. I don't know, I didn't think. I mean..." I sigh. "Just, thank you."

And I realize something in that instant. The curse did kill me. The magic stopped my heart.

But friendship brought me back to life. In the end, love did conquer the curse. Just not in the way I ever imagined it might.

"It's over," Cole whispers into my ear. "It's all over."

But as soon as he says those words, another face fills my vision. Sweet. Innocent. With green eyes that glimmer with the sunshine of a warm summer day. "No," I murmur, "it's not." Cole stiffens behind me, but I turn my attention to the faerie standing at the back of the room, crossing her arms and scowling at us. "And she's going to help us."

The faerie lifts her brows, as though silently asking, *who, me?* When I don't look away, she shakes her head. "No, I'm not."

"Yes, you are," I say, voice strong. I'm not the weak little girl I once was. I'm not going to be afraid of her. "I saved your life, you owe me."

She rolls her eyes, deepening her glare. "You just expedited the process. I was going to be fine."

"Are you sure about that?" I ask, tone as hard as stone, no longer delicate like a flower.

Her lips twitch into a frown as a wave of doubt passes quickly over her face. But when she replies, the bite is back. "Either way, I got out of the business of helping humans a very long time ago, when their greed murdered everyone I know. One act of kindness doesn't undo all the harm your people caused, all the lives they destroyed."

"What about helping me? My kind?" Cole adds softly.

The faerie winces, shifting her gaze toward him. Everything about her turns tender. The hard shell vanishes. "I'm sorry," she confesses. "I really am. What I did to you, I did out of desperation. Believe me when I say there was no other way. I never wanted to hurt you, but I needed magic and I needed it fast."

His eyes widen. "You're a priestess, aren't you?"

My jaw drops.

"All faeries have a little magic," she responds noncommittally. "But that's not the point. Yes, I borrowed your magic. Borrowed. The spell was going to run its course and the magic would have been returned to you no matter what. I left your magic alone and I left your parents' magic alone, so the three of you could still guide your people until that day came. I wasn't trying to hurt you."

"Well, my parents are dead, so your plan didn't really work out."

She purses her lips, releasing a deep breath. "I'm sorry for that. I am. But there are things I need to do, people I need to see. And I can't waste my time helping a human, least of all a human who possessed stolen magic, not when other people need me."

"Would it be a waste of time to break a curse?" I interject. "To free some magic? To give it back to those people you claim you want to help?"

Her eyes narrow. She turns to me, suspicion gleaming in those beautiful irises, which I now see are bright blue. "What do you mean?" she questions slowly, voice growing harder by the second. "Your magic is gone, otherwise I'd feel it."

"My curse isn't broken," I say simply.

"What?" Cole growls.

I grip his hand, shaking my head slightly. "It's not me. When I died, my magic transferred to an heir I didn't know was still alive." I lick my lips, throat tight as I recall her dirty, soot-covered cheeks, and her narrow, starved frame. "My sister. My little sister. My spirit traveled to her. I saw her. I saw the magic consume her. She inherited my curse. And I have to save her. I'd do anything to save her."

"I'll help," the faerie responds immediately.

Now it's my turn to be wary. "Why the sudden change of heart?"

She shrugs, crossing her arms and tossing her luscious blond hair over her shoulder. "I have a soft spot for children."

But there's a calculating gleam in her eyes, and I don't believe her words for a second—the newfound compassion is clearly a cover.

Yet before I can question her further, a man comes crashing through the front of the tent, stumbling on feet that have forgotten how to work.

"Cole?" he wheezes.

I know who he is even before Cole jumps to his feet, pulling the man in for a tight embrace.

One of the wolves.

One of his uncles.

Cole always said he looked just like his father, same hair, same eyes. But his smile, I realize now, that came from his mother. Because the grin spreading across his uncle's face is one I've seen dance across Cole's lips a hundred times before. He doesn't need to turn around for me to know it's there now, and I wouldn't want him to.

I want him to hold on to this moment.

To lose himself in it.

Because he's been waiting fifteen long years for this dream to come true. And I literally went to hell and back to give it to him.

Twenty-Seven

"Papa," I whisper.

For the first time in weeks, he eases his eyes open, blinking the fog away. The moment those dark, umber irises turn toward me, the world stops.

"Omorose?" he asks, voice scratchy and weak—yet so incredibly beautiful.

"Papa!" I cry, falling over him and wrapping my arms around his shoulders. "I was starting to think you'd never wake up."

He shifts, trying to hug me back I think, but he's too weak to really move. "What happened?"

I sit up, wiping my tears away as I dribble some water between his dry lips. "So much, I don't even know where to begin."

"The beast?" He coughs.

A smile pulls at my cheeks with the mere mention of Cole, and the way my father's brow pulls tight in suspicion doesn't go unnoticed. We can have this conversation another time, when he's a little healthier. The last thing I want to do is shock him to death by admitting I fell in love with the King of Beasts.

So I shake my head slightly, and instead reach down to grab his hand, moist with sweat and still a little warm with fever. "Papa," I murmur, "my magic is gone."

He gasps.

Immediately, a glow I haven't seen in a decade sparks to life in his eyes.

"That's not all," I say before he has time to comment. "Sissy is alive. I saw her, Papa. She's alive."

"Alive?" he whispers, voice cracking.

I can't even speak, my throat is closed tight, and my grin is no longer about Cole. It's about me, my family, and a sort of love I thought I had lost forever. So I nod and squeeze my father's hand tighter. And we stare at each other, not uttering a word, yet sharing more in that moment than I think we have in my entire life.

"Omorose?"

The soft question stirs my attention. I glance away from my father, looking over my shoulder to see Cole's head poking through the front of the tent.

"It's time."

I nod, turning back to the bed. "I have to go, Papa. But I'll be back soon to tell you everything. Go back to sleep, get some rest. And I'll be here when you wake up."

Before I've even finished speaking, his eyes have drifted closed. But now, his face is utterly at peace, not frowning with the torment of disease. He'll heal. Now that he knows everything will be all right, he'll be able to heal, eventually.

I brush my fingers through his hair, straightening it one more time, before I get up and leave, finding Cole right outside the tent. Immediately, his arm wraps around my shoulder, and I snuggle against his side.

It's hard to believe that little more than two weeks ago, we were surrounded by nothing more than wild animals and even wilder wilderness. But already, Cole's new kingdom is underway. Wooden frameworks for houses have started going up, some stone cottages are halfway built. Fires light the entire valley, which has been cleared of snow to make way for the construction. Children play in quiet circles while their parents work. Many of the women have banded together to tend to fragile fledgling gardens while the men grind away at the construction. Everyone is human, for the time being at least.

After I awakened the faerie and my magic vanished, the bubble of power blocking the electricity vanished too. Cole still had his magic, and so did his people, but for some reason it didn't obstruct the energy fields the way my stolen magic or the faerie's stolen magic did. Their power is more natural—it's not fighting for control at every moment, not charged by the constant battle for release. It's subtler, more nuanced. Just easier, like breathing. And I think that ease is what keeps it from interfering with the electricity.

When Asher and Jade returned to the base, saying that the bombs almost killed hundreds of innocent people who were now stranded in the mountains, tons of soldiers volunteered to help, needing some way to assuage the guilt. They brought tools and food and supplies. They brought medicine and doctors who treated my father. And some of them are still here now, building alongside Cole's people, helping resurrect the city they destroyed. And as long as the shifters remain in their human forms, no one suspects anything. We've had a few close calls in the cold hours of the night. But hearing a wolf howl to the moon isn't so unusual in these mountains—at least, that's what we told the visitors.

The faerie was a little harder to explain.

Even on a starless night, her skin somehow shimmers with sunlight. So we've mainly kept her out of sight.

Under extreme supervision.

Which is why four of Cole's uncles are stationed at each corner of her tent, blocking any possible chance of escape. They step aside as we enter.

"Finally, it's about time," she grumbles immediately.

I have to admit, I'm not going to miss her. At all. Not even in the slightest.

"My father woke up," I murmur, knowing that won't mean anything to her.

And it doesn't. After a brief pause, she crosses her arms, maintaining the same superior attitude. "Are you ready to do this or not? Because like I said before, there are plenty of other things I could be doing besides helping you."

"I'm ready," I hiss, annoyed. Two weeks with her were two weeks too many. And I can't wait for her to be gone so I can get some peace back in my life. Every second she's away is another second closer I am to having my sister again. "There's just one more thing we need to do before we let you go."

Her brows rise to sharp points.

Cole snarls under his breath behind me, copying my feelings exactly.

"A blood oath," I say, sounding a little more ominous than I intended.

She snorts. "A blood oath? Really? I already promised I would find your sister and bring her back."

I cock my hip, crossing my arms. "Forgive me if I don't believe you."

She sighs and rolls up her sleeve, baring one arm up to the elbow. "Let's get it over with then. I can't wait to leave this place, to go somewhere warm, somewhere I can feel the sun."

She does have a point.

But I sort of like the cold.

It's an easy excuse to keep Cole close, my own personal furnace. Even now, the warmth from his body presses into my back, blocking out the cold air leaking through the slits in the tent.

"Cole?" I murmur.

He understands, handing me his knife. I step closer to the faerie, unable to stop a little smile from twitching at the corners of my lips as I realize we're both staring at each other with the same look of mutual disgust. By now, I would have thought my frustration with her would have ebbed. After all, I've been in this tent countless times in the past two weeks, going over every detail of my sister's face that I could remember, planning how to get her back. I even let the faerie use a touch of magic to see into my mind and relive those last few moments of my life when the curse passed over, giving her every ounce of knowledge of my sister's whereabouts that I possess. Yet, for some reason, she just knows how to get under my skin and stay there.

When we're within arm's distance of each other, I stop, not getting any closer than I need to. And the way she's wrinkling her nose makes it clear she doesn't want me to come any closer anyway.

Gritting my teeth, I make a small cut across the palm of my hand and hold out the knife. She does the same. The moment we hold hands and the wounds touch, I sense the magic pulsing between us. A faerie blood oath is supposed to be an unbreakable bond, one Cole and I discovered in our research. But I never truly believed what I read until right now, feeling the power start to bind us.

"Do you swear to find my sister as soon as you can and to return her to me, unharmed, as quickly as you are able?"

The magic tightens, waiting. I hold my breath.

The faerie looks at me, raising one brow as though bored. "I swear to find your sister as soon as I can and to return her here to you unharmed as quickly as I'm able."

I don't let go. The tingle of magic washes over me, buzzing, standing each of my hairs on end. The faerie shakes out of my hold, wriggling free of my grasp with a frown on her lips.

Our hands fall apart.

But the touch of magic lingers.

An invisible tether crosses the space between us, tying us together. The oath. Instantly, the weight on my chest lightens. It worked.

"Anything else?" she remarks, voice dripping with sarcasm.

I lick my lips, pausing. Then I sigh. "Be kind to her, please. She's just a little girl who's all alone. And," I pause, and reach into the bag I dropped by the entrance of the tent, pulling out the old tattered bear that's comforted me so much in the past ten years. It's time to return Mr. Winky to my sister. He always belonged to her, and now she's the one who will need to be brave, who will need the comfort and strength a little piece of home might provide. "And give her this."

The faerie holds my gaze for a moment and I can't help but notice there is something sweet in her expression, something tender that I've never seen directed toward me before. But her eyes flick away, landing on Mr. Winky, and whatever I thought I saw vanishes. She uses her thumb and pointer finger to grab the little bear by the ear, holding him as far away as possible. And then, as always, she opens her mouth and completely ruins whatever little moment I thought we'd been sharing. "What in the world is this?"

I wince as he dangles precariously between us. He's already missing an eye, and I can just see the seam of his ear begin to rip. "My sister will understand," I say roughly, grabbing Mr. Winky and stuffing him into the faerie's bag before she has the chance to say no. "When you find her, just give him to her and tell her he's from me. Tell my sister that I love her and that I'm waiting and that I wish I could have gone with you. Tell her not to be afraid of the magic, tell her I know how to keep her safe. Please, just..."

I lose my words.

They're choked off by a lump in my throat.

A flicker of compassion passes over the faerie's face, a glimpse of the heart I know must exist somewhere inside of her. But then she flinches, as though annoyed with herself for softening even a little, even for a second.

"I'll be her fairy freaking godmother, okay?" the faerie snaps. And then she sighs, waving a hand over the front of her face and mumbling too quietly for me to hear.

Immediately, her body begins to fade, vanishing in midair. The room is empty.

The faerie is gone, as though she never existed in the first place.

"Did you know she could do that?" Cole asks, utterly confused.

I shake my head, glancing around the room, trying to find a trace of her. "No," I mutter, brows coming together tight. "If she could have left us the entire time, why did she stay? Why did she swear the oath? Why is she helping us?"

"I don't know." He sighs, reaching out to grasp my shoulders, turning me around so I'm looking into his eyes and not at the vacant room. "But she did," he urges. "She swore the oath. Everything will be all right."

I nod absently. "I just wish I could have gone with her. I hate that someone else is saving my sister. I hate that I'm not helping."

"Your father needs you here," he murmurs gently, cupping my cheeks, trying to soothe me with the timbre of his voice. And it works. A little. "Besides," he continues, "You saw what the faerie just did, you saw her magic. She's faster alone, without either of us helping. Your sister will be here before you know it, and by the time she arrives, we'll have figured out how to save her. We'll know how to break her curse."

I try to smile, but it doesn't work.

Because I want to believe him but I'm not sure I do.

"You never told me her name," he comments, trying to change the subject, to get me to think about something else.

"Eleanor," I tell him, voice heavy with all the worries I'm too afraid to say. "But we always called her Ella."

"Ella," he repeats, voice light, cheerful. Cole lifts my chin, trying to tug a grin out of me.

It doesn't work.

A moment later, I find myself swept up in his arms, unable to stop from laughing just a little.

"Cole! Put me down!"

"No," he replies easily, leaning down to press his lips against my neck, eliciting a soft sigh.

But then I remember who's right outside those doors.

And I have a feeling, even as humans, his uncles have the ears of wolves.

"Cole," I warn. "Put me down."

He purrs against my skin, making me shiver.

"Cole," I protest.

Weakly.

So weakly.

He continues dancing light kisses across my shoulder, up my neck, just below my ear.

"Cole…"

The word comes out as a sigh.

But then a soft chuckle makes its way through the slit in the tent, before fading into a cough.

"Cole!" I shout, fully alert, flinging myself from his arms. Before he can say or do anything, I jump out of the tent, cheeks burning with a blush. I keep my eyes on the ground below my feet, not making eye contact with anyone.

Behind me, a gruff growl breaks the silence of the day as the tent flap is thrown violently open. The slap of tarp is followed by some under-the-breath comments I don't quite catch.

"Tamed..."

"She-wolf..."

"Happens to the best of us..."

Cole roars. His uncles howl.

And before I realize what's happening, I've been tossed over a very broad shoulder, suddenly airborne again.

"Cole."

"Omorose."

"Cole," I repeat, voice harder.

He shifts, sliding me around so I'm nestled in his arms with my head pressed against his chest. And then he gruffly mutters, "I think I liked it better when we were alone."

But he's grinning.

And his smoky, gray eyes are streaked with those midnight-blue highlights I love so much. The sight of them steals the protest from my lips. So I wrap my arms around his neck, trying to ignore the gentle catcalling drawing everyone's attention to us. But my cheeks still feel on fire.

"Where are we going?"

He glances down at me with a look that sends heat all the way to the tips of my toes. "Somewhere with a little bit of privacy."

A delicious sort of anticipation builds, making my nerves go haywire, driving me wild. I have to look away because otherwise I'm afraid my inner she-wolf will emerge, making me want to maul him in front of everyone anyway. And I know in that moment, his uncles are wrong. I definitely didn't tame my beast. There's nothing tame or broken about us.

We set each other free.

I press my head against his chest, listening to his heart beat just a little bit faster with each passing moment, and I let him carry me away. Because I know I'll go wherever he wants to take me.

In these arms, I found a place where I belong.

In these arms, I know everything will be all right.

In these arms, I fell in love.

And I'm never letting go.

Don't miss

Chasing Midnight

Once Upon a Curse Book Three

The classic fairy tale of *Cinderella* gets retold—only this faerie isn't a godmother, she's a priestess, and it's not Cinderella she wants, it's her magic! Add one prince. Subtract one pumpkin. And don't forget the glass slipper…

Sign up at the below link to be notified the morning it goes on-sale!

TinyLetter.com/KaitlynDavisBooks

About The Author

Bestselling author Kaitlyn Davis writes young adult fantasy novels under the name Kaitlyn Davis and contemporary romance novels under the name Kay Marie.

Always blessed with an overactive imagination, Kaitlyn has been writing ever since she picked up her first crayon and is overjoyed to share her work with the world. When she's not daydreaming, typing stories, or getting lost in fictional worlds, Kaitlyn can be found indulging in some puppy videos, watching a little too much television, or spending time with her family.

Connect with the Author Online:

Website: KaitlynDavisBooks.com
Facebook: Facebook.com/KaitlynDavisBooks
Twitter: @DavisKaitlyn
Tumblr: KaitlynDavisBooks.tumblr.com
Wattpad: Wattpad.com/KaitlynDavisBooks
Goodreads: Goodreads.com/Kaitlyn_Davis